"Carlisle elegantly and evocatively de  Cabot, a peripatetic Boston Brahmin ...., .... ... g.... ....... ... thedral at the center of his tale, loses the ground under his feet. Amid wood-paneled walls, fine scotches, and expensive toys, Cabot slowly disassembles his spiritually burdened, privileged life. Carlisle offers his readers delicate meditations on interconnected themes, distributing his story into chapters reminiscent of Chopin's *études*. We glimpse faith in search of acts, privilege in search of duty, artifice in search of beauty, and ambition in search of purpose. Carlisle's timely and important book helps to frame today's social upheavals."

**—STEPHEN HARRIS**

Professor of English, University of Massachusetts Amherst

"A personal story of a young American thrown into the world of jealousy and greed in the Episcopal Church. Riveting, painful, and brilliant!"

**—DAVID STAINES**

Canadian literary critic, university professor, writer, and editor

"In his Gospel, Luke tells us that during the visitation, Mary tells Elizabeth that God 'has filled the hungry with good things: and the rich he hath sent away hungry' (1:53). This, it seems to me is, at the heart of Chris Carlisle's novel. Beautifully written and engaging, it tells a story of unadorned Christianity. Jeans, not collars. Feeding the poor. Housing the homeless. Christianity on the streets, in the manner of Jesus."

**—BARRY MOSER**

American Book Award-winning illustrator of *The Pennyroyal Caxton Bible, Alice in Wonderland,* and *A River Runs Through It*

"Here is a novel that will stick with you long after you've read it. Carlisle writes about worlds he knows . . . asking the quintessential questions about life's meaning and offering, among the witty and charged exchanges, a wealth of profound answers for the reader to ponder."

**—PAUL MARIANI**

National Book Award finalist, poet, author, professor, and biographer

"One of the best characters in Christopher Carlisle's *For Theirs is the Kingdom* is the city of Montreal. Westmount, the Old City, Place Ville Marie, Le Plateau, the Golden Mile—they all play a part in this story of a man's search for a fulfilling life path. Attorney Ben Cabot meets a sad bishop at Saint Joseph's Oratory atop Mount Royal and a renegade street priest on Place d'Youville, and finds that the church has been looking for God in all the wrong places."

—DICK TERESI

Coauthor of *The God Particle*, contributing writer to
*The New York Times*, *The Wall Street Journal*, and *The Atlantic*

# For Theirs Is the Kingdom

# For Theirs Is the Kingdom

Christopher Carlisle

RESOURCE *Publications* · Eugene, Oregon

FOR THEIRS IS THE KINGDOM

Resource Publications
An Imprint of Wipf and Stock Publishers
199 W. 8th Ave., Suite 3
Eugene, OR 97401

www.wipfandstock.com

PAPERBACK ISBN: 978-1-7252-9412-7
HARDCOVER ISBN: 978-1-7252-9413-4
EBOOK ISBN: 978-1-7252-9414-1

02/09/21

To Betsy,
magnificent mentor,
and matriarch

# 1

FOR ALL LIFE'S OPPORTUNITIES that are borne by accident, there are certain ones which come along that are destined to change us forever. Sometimes it's a person, sometimes it's a place, sometimes it's a circumstance that draws us down the river of life by ways we had never planned. It was only when I started to sense some fluvial destination—vaster still than the Amazon's fathomless vastness that flows to the sea—that a skeptic like me could entertain the possibility that there might be another life as abundant as this one has been.

As someone who questioned the destination for as long as he could remember, I took the chance only when realized I had no choice. Maybe because I was given to think I would always have a choice that I fell prey to the privileged illusion that I didn't have to make one. Even the accident of birth seemed no more an accident than the land of "manifest destiny" to which I chanced to be born.

Yet thanks to an unforeseen confluence on this river of accidents, I found myself washed onto the shore of Old Montreal. If for me it began on the River Charles, and for Hale, in the trout streams of Yorkshire—to carry us both by the tides of Saint Lawrence to the City of a Hundred Steeples—I now know that I would never be borne on the red winds of the Sahara until being baptized in a watercourse that wasn't of my own making. Because for Hale, God was not a metaphorical river; God was a literal river, flowing past the religious institutions that were crumbling on its shores.

As embarrassing as it is to admit, I grew up assuming that privilege was only for those who enjoyed it. I don't recall when I came to assume it—only that I did. But what I remember, as well as the name that christened me "Benjamin Cabot," is that there was a time when I believed the world was for everyone.

In a family for whom morality was a function of social position, I never considered the likelihood that we were part of the problem. It was not that the Cabots were hardhearted bastards who cast a cold eye on the poor. It was rather that our superior vision allowed for convenient blindness.

As the cliché goes, a boy could not have asked for better parents. Though in this rare case, the platitude happened to be true. As an only child whose parents had longingly wished him into existence, my strongest memory of those days was that life was an undeserved gift.

If the goodness with which my mother lived hers was not a figment of my imagination, neither was my father's eminence in the legal establishment. Fair-handed as he was in the worst of conflicts, his principles were absolute. And if his legal mind didn't damn the opposition, his standing did.

But Emma and I had an understanding that has carried me to this day. Referring to me as her "enfant terrible" for most of my schoolboy days, she never failed to come to my defense when the chips were down. The last intervention occurred in the kitchen of a high school elective, "Gourmet Foods"—when I failed to complete a spectacular pass of a loaf of bread I'd just baked—and Emma was summoned to what became known as "The Cabot Super-Bowl," where it was determined that it was time for Ben Cabot to graduate.

Only Emma could redeem my "deficit" as a fortuitous asset: "Your mind may be making too many connections, but the world isn't making enough." Undiagnosed was a related challenge with "spatial organization"—when I sensed I had to go in one direction, I knew I had to go in the other. Whether or not one accepted her view that the world was inclined to be wrong, it was safe to presume what her son thought was right was not the accepted wisdom.

This may have been why I envied my friends who were able to follow the rules. For all my justified complaints about religious institutions, I must admit that my row with the church was in truth an authority problem. As a faithful agnostic, it seemed to me that the God the church professed was not the sort who would have tolerated any institution.

It was my hours as a child in Emma's lap that will always be with me. Through long afternoons, she patiently fielded interminable questions about everything from *The Canterbury Tales* to *The Little Engine That Could*. In fact, I may have my mother to blame for the trouble that lay ahead—having introduced me to Chaucer's take on the hypocrisies of the church.

In any case, having Emma in my corner was no less than a schoolboy's blessing. Maybe my knack for making her laugh gave me shelter from the enemy. Adored by the world as Emma Cabot was—both as a person and a gifted author—my irreverent rants about the toadying types who tended to worship her, surely offered relief to someone who knew a forty-karat phony when she saw one.

On the other hand, I remember my father, paradox that he was, relating a joke defining the difference between a rich man and a poor one. "The rich man sleeps with a can-o-pee over his bed, while a poor man sleeps with one under." However grateful Ben Sr. was to have drawn the straw of advantage, I always sensed that poverty was a concern which was always with him.

The truth is, Ben Sr.'s branch of the Cabots was a bundle of contradictions. What may have appeared to fellow brahmans as "the ideal family" was in fact an eccentric, blue-blooded clan of utterly quixotic players. Yet I suspect that we were little different from any other family which believes itself to be so utterly normal that the rest of the world has to be crazy.

From a long line of Beacon Hill barristers reaching back to colonial times, it was probably why he could only imagine being a Democrat. So the "Middle Way" of the Episcopal Church couldn't have suited him better— that thinly veiled ruse conceived to obscure King Henry's liberal codpiece, which bore the mark of a compromise in order to safeguard the faith, while justifying a canonical route into the knickers of Ann Boleyn. I recall growing up believing that God was less an object of prayer than the subject at which the faithful took aim through the tines of a dinner fork.

Ben Sr.'s religious skepticism had less to do with God than with what he foresaw as the certain demise of the institutional church. While Senior Warden of our Beacon Hill parish, he was often heard to remark: "When is a businessman not a businessman? When he's a vestryman." As stalwart a churchman as he was, his faith always went unspoken—leaving his son to believe what he wished, so long as it was decent.

I was always aware that what I knew of myself was different from what the world saw. Even if the Cabots were indeed "eccentric," we had a pass to believe otherwise. Which may be why my genuinely "normal" fiancé jumped ship—having first glimpsed a promising future from the outside, looking in—giving me to fear that whatever kind of leader I might be, one day I'd turn around to see that no one was following me.

3

It wasn't until the river of life was rising into my thirties that the question of God seemed relevant enough even to warrant an answer. If it was true my peculiar brand of faith was no less than heresy, I felt reassured to know "heresy" was a judgment of the church. Yet if I'm bound to be burned at the stake, I have two priests to thank—one, an apostate man of God, and the other, a Wall Street cleric—because it took them both for me to make sense of the impossible question of God, and how the diabolical things that happened could ever be done in "His" name.

Before my first glimpse of Cathedral in the Night on the streets of Old Montreal—apart from a pirate birthday party that sank me when I turned eight—the only experience I'd ever had that might qualify as "religious" was a vocational crisis I brought to my father at the ripe old age of nine. I remember standing before my judge in our old-shoe living room. As I stuttered and stammered, and hemmed and hawed, I managed to convey that, with all due respect, I had decided not to go into the law.

With utmost regard for my fourth-grade wisdom, he asked what I had chosen to do. I will never forget his discerning eyes—as though nothing were of greater import. Cognizant that the larger world might not be prepared for my answer, I drew in a sigh, and managed to heave: "Protector of the Animals."

He pondered his young defendant's confession like the sagest of magistrates. Silence weighed in the living room as I waited out his judgment. "Ben," he said, and put his hand on my shoulder, "it sounds like a fine profession."

Attributing my vocational choice to the pigeons on the Esplanade, I recalled for him our family walks on Sunday afternoons. He too was distressed by the pigeon-abuse at the hands of the boys in the park—boys, I presumed without evidence, were spoiled, rich Beacon Hill kids. What he didn't know was that as we walked, I would name every one of them, then as if in a dream, would gather them up and fly away with them.

He asked if "Protector of the Animals" involved more than simply pigeons. As I rattled off every creature in the kingdom that was sure to demand my attention, I felt suddenly overwhelmed by the impossible magnitude of the task. Not unlike confronting the question of how Santa could deliver all those presents, I burst into tears, and he took me into his elegant gaberdine lap.

As my heaving abated, came my last appeal: "How—can I—possibly do it?"

"You can only do what you can," he said.

"What if—it's not enough?"

Considering the question, he made an offer I've always been unable to refuse. He looked me in the eye, and said: "Why don't you let me worry about that?"

And in that fleeting moment, everything changed—my fears, my tears, my desperation that the world was just too daunting—as though some greater presence bloomed in the room, thanks to his inexorable wisdom. If this greater presence was the presence of "God," it was one I'd never known in church. So, I was left to presume that "God" was at best an afterthought: an unsubstantiated rumination that no one really believed in.

To the extent this was my gravest crisis growing up, I had little to complain about. Apart from my alleged "authority problem," I was a pretty well-adjusted kid. Yet, as popular as I may have been in my halcyon days of college, law school commencement set the stage for the truth that I had no friends.

It was a U.S. Poet Laureate and Beacon Hill neighbor at the Cabot dinner table who opined the word "friend" was the most overused word in the English language. He went on to explain that those we call "friends" are most often "acquaintances"—a word, he believed, had to return to redeem this duplicitous time. A literary sage of unquestioned renown, he knew an acquaintance when he saw one; so, short of a challenge, I screwed up my courage and asked, "What makes a friend?"

I couldn't discern if his smile was stretched by the naiveté of my question, or by having to answer what he considered to be a self-evident fact. "When you are rock climbing," he said, "a friend is someone you would trust to set your piton. When it is your piton or his, hanging from a cliff, it is yours he would choose to set."

Recalling his first anthologized poem penned in the trenches of France, I was ready to listen as one who'd been spared the terror of mortal combat.

"That would leave us with very few friends."

"Very few," he said.

I will always regret that on that fateful cliff, I failed to set Hale's piton. What scares me is not the shame I would face if my failure came to light; what scares me is a world in which such failure is no longer shameful at all. To this day I wonder why some choose to see, while the rest of us avert our eyes—and justify our lives by self-serving explanations of some "greater good," never realized.

Of all the sins on the human palette, betrayal has to be the darkest. While my public excuse for going north was the "opportunity" it afforded, in truth it was an illicit rendezvous that commended a virgin start. But if I thought escape across the border meant an escape from treachery, I had another thing coming—if not another order of treachery.

When I told my father where I was going, Ben Sr. inscrutably smiled. At first I thought he was going to recall our "college visit" to Montreal, which served as an excuse in my waning high school days to be together in the sadness of that fall. Instead, he invoked a celebrated line from his literary muse, Samuel Clemens: "You know what Twain said about Montreal," he said.

He could see that I didn't.

"It's the only city where you can't throw a brick without breaking a church window."

I should have paid attention to what I dismissed as a light-hearted, passing remark. The trouble was, my father was one of those men who rarely got it wrong. Even when I thought he had missed the point, he always seemed to get it right—which was enough to make any firstborn son throw a brick through a stained-glass window.

What he couldn't predict was that it would be his son to throw the brick through the stained-glass window. Not that he would have expected less on the battlefield of litigation—because unlike himself, he knew I wasn't blessed with his legendary patience. It was rather that he knew that going to church was for me like watching paint dry, and that if any institution would escape my attention, it would have been the church.

So, days past turning thirty, and a mother's farewell dinner feting her unmarried son, I felt as though I was being shipped to summer camp, never to be heard from again. Posing as my own self-appointed chauffeur behind the wheel of a one-way rental car, I wondered if this town that had coddled me too long would continue to remember my name. I wondered if the shining Esplanade I watched disappearing in the mirror, blanketed by hundreds of imaginary pigeons whose names I vowed to recall, would welcome me back as its native son with the grace by which I was received, or if the foreign city to which I was going meant never coming home again.

With nostalgic memories drawing me north to magnificent Montreal, I looked forward to returning to what stayed in my mind as a uniquely cosmopolitan city. And fleeing my pathetic amorous disaster, and the arms of my beloved hometown, I was ready to turn to another horizon that might lead me toward truer north. So, as I crossed the bridge to Ville Marie, set like a jewel on top of the world, I already sensed that somewhere in that place was something I was looking for.

# 2

IF DESTINIES ARE ACCIDENTS, however well-disguised as shattered fortunes luckily redeemed, mine had run the rails of an inauspicious tryst and an auspicious coincidence of birth. My father's lineage, and his advice to acquire dual-nationality, granted me Canadian citizenship and the right to work without a visa. When my firm was retained for long-term legal counsel to a company in Montreal, I was the last man standing both fluent in French and free to leave on the next train.

Rather than fall prey to the overworked illusion of love in a foreign city, I purposefully resisted the hope that every corner turned on some romantic destiny. Having always imagined Montreal as Europe without the cost of an airline ticket, I looked forward to taking in its energetic air, and expelling the fumes of the past. To sweeten the deal, the firm bankrolled the lease for an elegant furnished townhouse, several blocks north of the Golden Mile and ten minutes from the downtown office.

From the evening I arrived, Montreal offered me a late-night walker's paradise. Residing as I did on an iron-gated lane lined with diplomats and politicians, I quickly learned the quirks and eccentricities of this culturally schizophrenic town. For two hundred years Montreal was governed by British magistrates, and only recently had the Quebecois French risen to their rightful power.

The separatist sixties were a decade gone, and prosperity was in the air: glass towers soaring high above Victorian houses slated for downtown demolition. Mount Royal loomed behind these human ambitions as though it deserved its prideful name, graced by limestone manses and manicured green lawns in the most fashionable quarter of the city. My own brick Georgian townhouse was tucked between McGill and the Anglo-beginnings of Westmount, hosting aristocracy both feigning to be landed and pretending to be "bilingual."

As comfortable as Westmount immediately felt, beginning with my first sortie, I was immediately drawn south to the Saint Lawrence and the land of tea and oranges. And there was the Old City as I remembered it, in its stoic, stone abandonment. I wished my father had been there to recollect together the beauty the two of us had seen—perhaps to help me look ahead to where I was going by resurrecting where we had been.

Lured as I was by its European grandeur, there was a sadness in the air: a lavish, barren woman beyond her fertile years, when she could have given birth to a kingdom. Still, I sensed the solitary stirrings of my youth, and the stuff of yet more ancient dreams. Still I looked ahead to some retrospective future—to the European ticket unredeemed.

In those days the Old City was as hollow as a drum when the grand banks closed at four o'clock. Unlike those that shed their granite fenestration for the drive-up architecture of the suburbs, the domed magnificence of the Bank of Montreal held its sacred ground in the bourse. Empty Catholic convents had gone the way of the limestone livery stables, and monumental warehouses, street after street, made for weathered washboards of neglect.

It was here that I chanced upon "Cathedral in the Night." I remember the Sunday evening in October when I stood on the Basilica steps—mystified by the plume of light across the deserted city square. Luminous leaves in the yellow urban trees held the heady musk of autumn as I traversed Place d'Armes, and came upon that curious cloud of light.

Drawing near, I surveyed a crowd of people who looked to have spontaneously gathered under an incongruous industrial light one might see on a construction site. In the midst of the crowd, before two folding tables, stood a young, wiry, shorthaired tough, who was standing in front of a loaf of bread, a cup, and a wooden cross filled with burning candles. In the absence of liturgical accoutrements, not to mention material walls, it nonetheless evoked a sanctuary, uncannily made of light.

Hearing "The Last Supper" in perfect French, I was taken by the fluid reenactment, as impromptu the leather-backed celebrant recounted the betrayal of Jesus. He took a loaf of bread and broke it high above his head. Solemnly scanning the motley crew before proclaiming it "The body of Christ!" he declared that the table was not his, nor theirs, but "God's"—and therefore it was everyone's.

Lifting the cup, he ritually explained the purported "wine" was grape juice. While the bread was being passed, steam tables rolled out under the power of assistants; and the aromatic meal, wafting through the air, made it worthy of its billing as a supper. As the chalice circulated, I withdrew from the light, knowing that I didn't belong—breathing a thankful sigh of relief into the anonymity of night.

Because for me, as for most of my peers, the church was at best irrelevant. And for some of us, trusting the church was like trusting the fox to mind the henhouse. Even my own denomination's righteously liberal tradition ironically owed its pledge to the poor to a history of millionaires.

To this day I wonder if, along with my plight of social isolation, it was that cloud of light that moved me to darken the door of the Anglican Cathedral. The Book of Common Prayer had always succeeded in giving me a splitting headache, and the only thing I dreaded more than the sermon was the styrofoam cup coffee hour. Like every other kid who'd been made to go to church by parents who were made to do the same, at twelve I became a "confirmed Episcopalian": I only went to church at Christmas.

But being a stranger in an alien land can lead one to do stranger things. In a foreign country of expatriates and exiles—where past regrets can rear their ugly heads to threaten one's very undoing—my work as a mergers and acquisitions lawyer which had come to justify my life felt progressively like embezzlement from an increasingly indebted future. Concerned that along with my sense of purpose, I might also be losing my mind, against my better judgment, several Sundays before Christmas I attended Christ Church Cathedral.

For me the greatest blessing of the eight o'clock service was its habit of being short. I guessed that this one's protracted length had to do with the pomp and circumstance which was triggered by the diocesan Bishop being in attendance. Out of respect, I obediently stayed in my pew for his final benediction—resisting the urge to make my escape, and lining up to greet him.

In the narthex he didn't appear as tall as he had under the Bishop's miter. His spray of flaxen hair, less the soaring headgear, defied a man who must have been sixty. Peering through classic horn-rimmed glasses to scrutinize the stranger, he unexpectedly stretched a rubbery smile that immediately emanated warmth.

"And who are you?" he welcomed me—around a Yorkshire accent.

"Ben Cabot," I intoned—phonetic Bostonian.

"Greetings!" he declared, gripping my hand. "What brings a Yankee this far north?"

I might have hesitated.

"You didn't come to Montreal by accident!" he said.

"Legal problems," I quipped.

He quizzically peered.

"I'm a lawyer," I confessed.

"Glad to hear the problems aren't yours!"

I laughed. "Not the legal ones."

"Do you have a card?"

I thought he was kidding.

"I could use a barrister!"

Seeing he was serious, I drew one out and handed it to him.

"I'll give you a ring!"

But before I could respond, he was lost in a swarm of congregants.

# 3

ON TUESDAY MORNING I picked up the phone to the lilt of a librarian. Introducing herself as "the Bishop's Assistant," she proposed a meeting for Thursday. Since the University Club was only blocks from my office in the Place Ville Marie, at five I descended the cruciform tower and walked to my destination.

The hundred-year-old club discreetly stood a stone's throw south of Sherbrooke, quietly defying the gleaming towers that scraped the Golden Mile. Tentatively climbing the carpeted steps to the subdued Victorian door, I prepared to enter a British Empire on which the sun never set. A tightly nostriled Brit at the Maitre D' stand looked to be expecting me, and before the "p" in "Bishop" had popped off my lips, he was already brandishing his arm.

Taking his lead, I followed him down the hall to a library, where ensconced in a damask wingback chair sat the Bishop in a shooting jacket. Gentry got up with his infectious smile and extended a hearty hand, revealing a collarless purple shirt and pectoral cross draped to the pocket. At the Bishop's bidding, I sat down in a matching wingback chair facing his, while the nostriled Maitre D' seamlessly replaced himself with a white-gloved assistant.

"What will you be having, Sir?" our man inquired—to say the Bishop's choice had been made.

I looked across at Gentry.

"I'd suggest the Glenlivit."

"Glenlivit," I deferred to my host.

"You don't want to take the matter under advisement?"

"I've been doing that too long," I said.

"Where do you call home?"

"Boston," I imparted.

"Great town—next to Montreal!"

"You might be right," I granted.

"Do you have people here?"

"Only in Toronto," I said.

"Toronto was my first cure as a priest," he said.

"You didn't stay," I remarked.

"The English are insufferable," Gentry retorted, his Yorkshire accent ringing in my ear.

The white gloves returned and laid down the Scotch.

"And what brings you to Montreal?" he asked.

"Work," I informed him.

"There must be work in Boston!"

"I guess I was ready for a change."

"What sort of change?"

I pondered the question. "The kind that turns a life around," I said.

In retrospect it wasn't like me to confess my personal life to a stranger—let alone to a Bishop who, despite my skepticism, could bring the fire of judgment down on me. Perhaps it was his ease, and manifest disinterest in the particular details, which gave me to trust his best intentions in welcoming me to Montreal. Nevertheless, I only cryptically alluded to Leilah's game-changing conduct that moved me to consider this very different life from the one I was living.

"Repentance!" Gentry said.

If the truth were known, just hearing the word made me cringe.

"That's what repentance means," the Bishop pronounced. "From the Greek, it means 'to turn around.'"

"I've never been big on repentance," I admitted.

"Who the hell is?" he came back.

Mildly surprised, I decided to come clean: "Nor that big on going to church."

"You're in good comp'ny!"

"What was that?" I asked.

"You're in good comp'ny," he repeated. "I've always preferred the out-of-doors to falling asleep in a pew."

Gentry defied every stereotype of a cleric I had ever suffered. Exuding worldly confidence, embracing ambiguity, putting authority at risk, upended everything I had assumed was required of a self-respecting Bishop.

"I still wonder," he went on, "if I became a priest so that I didn't have to listen to the sermon."

I laughed. Though I surely sympathized with the sentiment, I didn't expect it from the preacher. The only service I'd ever attended that proved to be worth the trip was to a Black Baptist church in Alabama, which I attended with my roommate, Earlie Sanders.

After I discovered Leilah's affair with the captain of the tennis team, Earlie decided that what I needed was a Sanders family Thanksgiving. Unbeknownst to me, the Wednesday night before was a "Service of Prayer and Praise." Having once endured "African-American Sunday" at my parents' church—where I was given to assume that "Amazing Grace" was written to be sung by the Queen—for the first time I realized that hymns could send chills up and down the human spine, and that faith could be as real as the unbridled joy which filled that little wooden church.

"What's the sound of one hand clapping?" I nudged Earlie after the service. Earlie grinned. "It's the same sound as Episcopalians putting two hands together."

Earlie laughed. It was the kind of laugh that left little doubt about how Earlie Sanders was raised. For all my regrettable profanity in our three years of living together, I never heard Earlie so much as say "crap"—and true to form, he replied, "Ben, it's all good!"

Risking stereotype, I recall asking Earlie why the Black church had so much more "spirit." He took it in the ingenuous way I had intended it. And then he said, "Maybe because God always stands on the side of the oppressed."

As I looked across at Gentry with Scotch in hand, I admit it was no small feat to get past the images of God as "King" to one who stood with the oppressed. It wasn't that I was oblivious to the suffering Jesus had endured. It was rather that his suffering was so glorified that it hadn't seemed like suffering at all.

"How do you think Jesus would have done in church?" I abetted my gracious host.

"If you mean the synagogue," Gentry came to life, "he was always in trouble! He silenced congregations. And it was pissing off the priests in the Temple that got him killed!"

As vaguely aware as I may have been of Jesus's cantankerous nature, I'm sure I assumed that at the bottom, he was an institutional man. I had never entertained that his rhetorical tares were about institutional religion.

In that moment I imagined Jesus in the Temple, praying for the sermon to be over—and dreaming of a field where the lilies needn't spin for the world to dwell in all its glory.

"Speaking of pissing off the powers that be, I've pissed off a few of my own." Asking me to call him Stephen, he beckoned the waiter for another round. Courted by the city and developers, the trustees of the diocese had been approached about a metro station under the Cathedral, and a "sky-scraper" on the campus grounds.

"What are the terms?"

"Four million a year—on a ninety-nine-year lease."

"That's a tidy sum."

"The Trustees would agree. I'm the one with the problem."

To be honest, I wasn't sure why it was a problem. To me it seemed like fortuitous luck—if not "a movement of the Holy Spirit." Presuming liberal politics were in Gentry's genes as much as they were in my own, I was surprised to learn that the ills of capitalism had little to do with it.

"Look, I'm a Torey," Gentry said, "but no man can serve two masters."

"Most of us serve only one," I lamented. "Unfortunately, not yours."

"Ours," he amended.

"Fair enough," I said. "Does it matter where the money comes from?"

"No more than where Judas got his money," he replied.

"What do the Trustees think?"

"Without the money, there would be no church."

"Do you disagree?" I asked.

He considered the question. "Without the money, there would be no institution."

"And with it?" I retorted.

"With it . . ." Gentry said. "With it there may be no church."

When a sonorous clock struck the hour of seven somewhere in a distant room, Gentry abruptly cut to the chase and landed his impending request. He wanted to know his fiduciary powers according to canon law, but didn't want to show his hand to the public until it was necessary. Asking me to bill my working hours to "Stephen Gentry, private citizen," I told him to treat it as pro bono work—as "part of my Cathedral pledge."

"Your pledge would be going to divide the house," he graciously declined the offer. "And according to Christ, a house divided against itself cannot stand."

Leaving the Club, we climbed Mansfield together and paused at the corner of Sherbrooke. He promised to send over the relevant files and canons to my office. I asked if he could wait until after Christmas, and for the first time he looked relieved.

When I thanked him for the drink, he shrugged it off, as though there would be more to come. Plunging his hands into his shooting jacket, he energetically started down Sherbrooke. "Where tha's muck, tha's money!" he called—and he disappeared into the night.

# 4

GOING HOME FOR CHRISTMAS, I returned to a city I had never remembered as small. Though Boston was larger on the demographic sheet, as I strolled around Beacon Hill, it lacked the expansiveness that stretched the international streets of Montreal. Not unlike a favorite college sweater inadvertently put into the dryer, in a matter of hours my boyhood home had me feeling claustrophobic.

I suddenly felt as if I were back in John F. Kennedy Park, with Brooks and Leilah at it in the dark like Leda and the goddam Swan. The truth is, the trouble between Brooks and me began before the affair. Following our season celebration at the end of my junior year—having just won the Ivy League trophy at the tennis center named for Brooks's father—Brooks decided to host a bash at the Harvard Club downtown, to which Earlie and the other scholarship players were somehow not invited.

That was my last day on the Harvard tennis team. Of course, Earlie took it entirely in stride—"Ben, open your eyes!"—but I no longer had the heart for it, and was happy to have left them all for good. What I didn't know was that in the process, Leilah's heart left for good, only to be found in Kennedy Park, exposed to the starry sky.

Engaged to be married after commencement and before law school in the fall, I will never forget my mother's infuriating silence about the engagement. Unlike my father, for whom silence always meant the decision was mine to make, Emma Cabot, however generous, knew trouble when she saw it. On a hunch from a chum, I was witness to Brooks, sprawled out in his grass-stained khakis: caught in a late-night "torrid embrace," with Leilah's undies in a flutter.

When I got back to my room, Earlie was at his desk, hitting the books. Looking up to see his roommate in shock, he predictably dropped everything. I should have known Earlie wouldn't be surprised by the identity of the culprit—having also endured our white-kneed captain for three interminable years—so when he heard it had something to do with ground strokes and a fellow player's balls, he simply shook his head as though he had already seen the movie before.

I will always be filled with gratitude for people like Earlie Sanders, who, with nothing to gain, seem always to be there to see a friend through troubled waters. Nor will I forget my pirate birthday party which my mother threw for me when I turned eight—a swashbuckling brigand celebration that would have put Captain Hook to shame—or how, when the last buccaneer went home with his treasure bag of party favors, I quietly withdrew to our diminutive garden, sat down, and began to weep. When my mother came out and asked me what was wrong, all I managed was, "I don't deserve it": a plea which, thanks to this river of life, still bears an untold abundance.

Following a midday Christmas dinner, and several hours before my train, my mother rushed off to the Vincent Club to host its yuletide fete. Ben Sr. suggested that we retreat to the pocket-sized living room, awkwardly squeezed into our renovated carriage house built two hundred years before. Going to the sideboard, Ben Sr. poured two unsolicited ports—passing one to me before sitting down behind his shabby ottoman.

As he stretched his legs and released his tie from the clutches of a starched oxford shirt, I realized that at sixty, Ben Cabot, Sr. was a handsome son of a bitch. For the myriad times I'd cringed in response to being my father's "dead ringer," I suddenly felt like a cheap imitation from a second-rate generation. Though he frequently observed that men had two ears and one mouth—and so should listen twice as much as they should speak—at that vulnerable moment what I needed most was his sage paternal counsel.

"I always wondered how you kept your private life—private," I randomly implored.

He peered, as though he hadn't expected the question—or even the observation. Looking out the window, he finally remarked, "I must have felt that it was none of their business."

Steeling myself, I cut to the chase: "Sometimes I feel like a fake."

Before he could respond, came my second admission: "I wish you had given me your patience."

"What patience is that?"

"Yours!" I said.

"Don't believe everything you read."

"I don't," I insisted.

Ben Sr. looked at me. "We grew up in very different times. In my generation, one didn't have much choice but to keep a stiff upper lip. At the risk of romanticizing yours," he said, "you have a lot more freedom."

"Freedom to do what?"

My father winked. "I'll look forward to hearing."

In his inimitable way, Ben Sr. let me know this was all he was going to say. As silence shrank the room, he drew a sip of port, and said, "Ben, I'm packing it in."

"Retiring?" I jumped.

Peering through his glasses, he said, "You didn't hear it from me."

"What does mom think?"

"She wants to move to Maine."

"What do you think?" I pursued him.

"No man on his deathbed ever wished he'd spent more time at the office."

"Not even you?"

My father smiled. "Not even me," he said.

"What will you do?"

He looked at me. "Maybe visit you," he said.

"I wish you would—as long as I'm there."

"Wherever you are," he said.

Our mythic weekend in Montreal bloomed in the living room. Though I had already decided to attend my father's alma mater across the Charles, by a family twist of fate I had the chance to attend McGill for free. Thanks to the marriage of an ancestral widow to a fur trader named James McGill, I was entitled to a gratis education at an illustrious university.

That trip revealed a side of my father that I had never seen before. I vividly recall his boyish excitement at the European spectacle, from every bohemian hole-in-the-wall bistro to the ballroom of the Ritz. So, as I took in the unanticipated news of my father's sudden retirement, I conjured a reprise of that memorable weekend—if only to be with him again.

I suggested a walk on the Esplanade before my mother's return. As empty as it was on Christmas day, the pigeons kept to themselves; though I found myself compulsively naming each of them all along the Charles. At last, I asked if he remembered my vocation as "Protector of the Animals"— and he wistfully smiled, before he replied: "How could I forget?"

As we turned back, I stopped him in his tracks: "Why did you become a lawyer?"

He gazed across the river. "I suspect because my father . . . and his father . . . were lawyers."

I didn't respond.

"I'm afraid we didn't give you much choice," he repented.

"I had a choice," I said. "I chose not to be a Protector of the Animals."

He smiled. "It still sounds like a fine profession. I wish . . . I had thought of it."

My suitcase was packed and sitting at the door when my mother returned from her party. Disappearing to the pantry, she came back with her trademark "college survival kit": typically, smoked oysters, cheese, assorted nuts, chocolate, and a bottle of sherry. Her parting admonitions brought the liberal use of her favorite appellation, "Darling"—anticipating the loss of her son to Canadian parts unknown.

As the train was pulling out of North Station, I watched them standing on the platform, my mother poignantly waving at me as though she could bring me back. With my father's arm draped around her shoulder in what I knew was a tender embrace, I tried to discern which of the two was holding the other one up. And I thought of how "tristesse" said it so much better than the English word, "sadness"—while I quietly acknowledged the possibility that I no longer had a home.

# 5

BETWEEN CHRISTMAS AND NEW Year's, most of the city's corporate offices were closed: their silver-haired directors ensconced in their homes, leaving downtown to younger men. Having received a load of firewood before I left for Boston, by the week's end a ghostly pile of bark was all that remained. With my feet to the fire, and my head marinated in ecclesiastical law—mixed with a shot of building code, and a little more than that of Christmas cheer—I immersed myself in this ironic commitment to the Bishop of Montreal, hoping I was undertaking an endeavor that might even qualify as worthwhile.

In the evenings I set out to resurrect the walks I imagined having taken with my father. For all my uncertainty about where we had gone, what stayed with me on those retrospective treks was a nostalgic awareness that this was the only time we had ever been alone. As well as I knew how he loved my mother, and hated being apart, I sensed somewhere down deep, there braved a longing boy with hopes that had never been fulfilled.

I found it strange that since returning from Boston, I reminded myself of an orphan. Freshly reassured of my parents' devotion to their first and only son, in those following days I felt increasingly aware that I didn't have a home. I wondered if the catch in Ben Sr.'s throat—"I wish . . . I had thought of it"—revealed a crack in the sure foundation of an illustrious Cabot tradition.

Mount Royal was cast in preferential darkness on the eve of returning to work. Lavish wreaths draped with burgundy ribbon graced the limestone manses, exuding elegant Georgian restraint and spills of buttery light. From Belvedere Circle I gazed down on the towers, like space stations rising in the night—threatening municipal building regulations that defended the mountain's height.

# For Theirs Is the Kingdom

Phantoms of regret for my star-crossed engagement had chased me back to Montreal. On my solitary walks, I was comically reminded of my first romantic encounter, when as a junior high Don Juan, I phoned a short-lived "steady" with a list of conversational prompts—and following several promising replies to my carefully rendered questions, I discovered I was speaking to a giggling friend who had been handed the telephone. However naive I was to believe that no one would do such a thing, at least it prepared me for Brooks's grass-stained khakis, grinding away in the night.

Descending to Sherbrooke, and heading east along the campus of McGill, I turned south at the gate, where aesthetic moderation gave way to the boasts of finance. A three-story wreath shimmered above a Palladian portico, while the Christmas tree gracing the Place Ville Marie shone like an overturned diamond. Feeding my lifelong fixation on Paris, my eyes were inevitably drawn to the Banque Nationale de Paris—rakishly angled out to the street.

But navigating south on Rue Saint Laurent across former Dorchester Street, I felt as though I'd gone from the land of the living to the land of the living dead. Like an obsolete furnace that burned itself out before the advent of prosperity, the quartier looked more like a spent combustion chamber than a habitable neighborhood. In doorways, homeless men stirred like embers before turning to sleep again—suggesting in a chance and ill-fated moment, they might as easily have turned to ash.

Randomly, I wondered whether Jesus had deliberately chosen to be homeless, or if he was a victim of the selfsame system that put these guys out on the street. Then I found myself neurotically obsessing about the pigeons on the Esplanade—and how, when taken from their nesting boxes, they would fly hundreds of miles to be home—bringing to mind Christ's curious identification with the animal kingdom, saying foxes had dens, birds had nests, but he had nowhere to lay his head. As biblically illiterate as I was, I don't know how the hell I missed it: that when he said the poor would always be with us, he was talking about himself.

Unlike most of us, who had been scattered by the winds of professional ambition, after graduation Earlie went back to Montgomery, Alabama. When he declined full-rides to the top law schools in the country, I had to ask him why. He looked at me as though I'd grown another ear, and he said, "Ben, I'm going home!"

Climbing Saint Laurent from Saint-Antoine on Sunday afternoon at dusk, I joined the festive flow of holiday tourists streaming toward Place

Jacques Cartier. Hotel de Ville stood proudly at the crest, like Napoleon with height: flaunting mansard roofs and gables, lighted gray stone turrets, and balconies bowing to the night. Descending the plaza, the ambient glow dissolved in the blackness of the river—yet strangely illumined by what came into view as a familiar cloud of light.

The diaphanous curtain surrounding the gaggle of ragged partici-pants mystically emitted a reminiscent aura in this new itinerant location. As I approached, and the gossamer fantasies of distance disappeared, the electric florescence made eerily surreal the horizontal cross in the night. Roughly translated, the celebrant called out: "At this cathedral, we don't want your money!"

Good thing, I thought.

"We want more than that—we want everything you've got!"

As a basket was passed, the community was asked to take a wooden token, on which, he explained, was inscribed a commitment the recipi-ent was asked to make. Naming several—sobriety, compassion, patience, forgiveness, hope—he dismissed as "mere collateral" the money that was normally put into an offering plate. Leery as I was of religious ritual for its inherent self-righteousness, there was nonetheless spare room for my own self-righteousness in this land of cowboys and priests.

By right, the celebrant should have been ordained, but given his mani-fest charisma, as well as his ability with one tough crowd, he didn't seem to fit the bill. His energy even justified the claim of Communion as a "cel-ebration"—expanding the night with an illogical hope that contradicted the surrounding drear. But when his arms went in the air, pronouncing "The Peace," and the dreaded shaking of hands, I quietly withdrew from that transitory light, to what I believed was safety.

# 6

GETTING EVEN WITH THE work that had accumulated over twelve idle days of Christmas, I managed to complete my review of the file and phone the Bishop's office. At first I was told he was out of town, but after being asked my name, the voice on the other end explained that she would have to call me back. In fifteen minutes, I had an appointment—"Though the Bishop was not to have been in"—coming as close to an apology as a British secretary came.

The diocesan offices were housed in what I guessed had been the Bishop's residence, where I met the undoubted incarnation of the voice that had lilted on the phone. Attractive in the way of a librarian, she was cordial for a British subject—rising to greet me with an outstretched hand, and even the threat of a smile. With pleasantries dispensed, she ushered me into a paneled reception hall, featuring a fireplace generous enough to accommodate a family of four.

When we arrived at the far end, my escort gingerly knocked on a pocket door. After a moment, the door slid open. There in a Brooks Brothers suit stood the Bishop, who amicably greeted me before thanking his assistant with a deferential smile, and sliding the door behind me.

Walls of books lined the office. Absent were the trophies I would have expected a hunter like Gentry might display; only a handsome Golden Retriever betrayed the scent of an outdoorsman. Her intelligent eyes darted to the Bishop's in search of her master's permission—but ignoring the plea, Gentry motioned to the pair of chairs in front of a hearth.

"I take none of the credit," Gentry nodded. "She was a made-dog when I got her. If I commanded her to sit at Sherbrooke and Crescent at nine o'clock in the morning, when I returned at five in the afternoon, there she would be, still waiting."

"Would that were the case with people," I said.

He invited me to sit. "It would be a great job if it weren't for the parishioners," he said. "What did you find out?"

"Which version do you want?" I asked, sitting down.

"The true one. It's been a while."

"As you know, as with every other church, the diocese owns the Cathedral. And as Bishop, you have almost absolute power—in every matter but property."

He saw what was coming.

"No matter how I sliced it, it's the Trustees' call."

If Gentry had been a man to sigh, I'm sure he would have done it. Getting up, he went over to a leaded window that looked onto the rear of the Cathedral.

"So, I'll be looking up at the Tower of Babel."

"You could reason with the Board," I said.

"They've heard enough from me."

"Are you sure they're wrong?"

Gentry wheeled around. "The first time the Cathedral went into the red, and they were grousing about 'legacy,' a Trustee explained the fourth Wise Man was forgotten because he didn't bring a gift."

Master of irony that Gentry was, I detected an apocryphal tale. Gentry was a bundle of contradictions: an Englishman who couldn't tolerate the English; a Bishop who couldn't abide the church; and a well-heeled conservative with unexplained convictions about the plight of the poor. However conflicted Gentry may have been by his seeming ambiguities, something in the weight of those ominous days suggested an ulterior motive.

"Four million a year would certainly ensure the Cathedral's future," I offered.

"What future is that?"

"The material one."

"Free money isn't free," he said.

Turning back to the window, he gazed out at the mooning apse of the Cathedral.

"What does it matter?" I finally asked.

"You tell me," he came back.

"In my profession, it wouldn't matter."

"Nor in mine," Gentry said.

As he stood at the window, like a captain looking out from the deck of his drydocked ship, I felt out of my depth—a freshman in a senior-level class I knew nothing about. When the silence went too long, I braved the question: "Why should the church be any different?"

"If it isn't," he replied, gazing through the window, "then what the hell is the point?"

The truth is, he was asking at least the wrong person—if not the wrong generation.

"We used to believe in a scandalous God. Now, the church is the scandal."

"Scandals of the church, I'm familiar with. I'm not sure about 'the scandal of God.'"

"Because you've heard it from us. A homeless God? It doesn't get much more scandalous than that.

"We've become a second-rate club," Gentry said. "And we don't even have a golf course."

He turned around. "Before the Roman Empire, being Christian meant choosing to be poor. Then we took the money. And when we did, it literally changed everything."

"You said it mattered where Judas got his money."

"Whence comes 'blood money,'" he said.

"I always thought that was a mafia term."

"What's the difference?" Gentry said. "If it is true that blood is thicker than water, money is thicker than blood."

There was something about Gentry's principled convictions that I realized was missing from my own. If at first I assumed his discouragement was a struggle with his legacy, I wondered if it was that he suddenly saw that the church was doomed to fail. Perhaps this explained the disparity between Gentry and my generation: we had never expected the church to be different from any other institution.

On the other hand, Gentry was different from everything I'd known about the church. If his life had become a caricature of a time already gone, there remained some constant which refused to yield to the likes of any institution. In any case, as a thorough-going pragmatist honed on the strop of Harvard Law, I was already scheming on behalf of a man I'd inadvertently come to believe in.

"There may be other ways to skin the cat," I offered a last pragmatic counsel. "Though the property legally belongs to the Trustees, politically it could be yours. If you went to court, you would probably lose—but on the front page of the Montreal Gazette. You're still the Bishop, and as long as there's resistance, the deal would be difficult."

"Resistance from whom?"

"It would probably have to come from the Cathedral."

"The Dean," Gentry said.

"Isn't he retiring?"

"We're searching for a new one as we speak."

"When will he be chosen?"

"It depends on the committee."

"The committee?"

"The committee," Gentry said. "Those who alone can do nothing, and together decide that nothing can be done."

"That sounds like a very long time," I said.

"Or not long enough," Gentry said.

# 7

IT MUST HAVE BEEN the end of January when Gentry called to have a drink. Holed up as I'd been, it was a welcome invitation I eagerly accepted. Apart from my daily expeditions from the townhouse to Place Ville Marie, I found myself making monumental attempts to deny the great out-of-doors.

Between the mountain and the river, Montreal epitomized unintelligent design—creating the greatest snowmaking machine known to the natural world. Snow banks piled so high one was apt not to see his next-door neighbor until spring, gave forays on foot the vicarious sensation of an Olympic bobsled run. On ropes attached to buildings up the steep incline of University Street, students persevered for their scholastic lives against the bitter squalls from the mountain.

Montreal women striding up Mansfield like svelte arctic pioneers reminded me "political correctness" did not apply to mink, or fox, or beaver. Sidewalks waxed with salt kept the frozen concrete ambiguously damp, inspiring me to pray for my pedestrian life—or a fortuitous hockey stick. Already grateful to Hydro Quebec for the anticipated warmth of the Club, I remember thinking if the cold didn't get me, the snowplows undoubtedly would.

Taking off my coat, I was shepherded back to an aromatic smoking room, where Gentry was surrounded by a blue-blooded band of erudite gentlemen. On seeing me, the Bishop waved me over and invited me into the fold. Introduced to "a fellow fisherman," I was immediately privy to the casting virtues of a bamboo rod his wife had given him for Christmas.

But with a handshake he was gone with the rest of them, and Gentry caught the waiter's attention. Holding up two fingers, he led the way to a duo of club chairs in the corner. Halfway there, he cast a line across his shoulder: "I need a Bostonian!"

"You've come to the right place," I said, sitting down.

"Or you, to the wrong one," Gentry said. "What do you know about Boston churches?"

"I know more about the bars," I confessed.

"A true Episcopalian—wherever you find four, you'll always find a fifth," he said. "Is your dad a churchman?"

I told him he had been the Senior Warden of our Beacon Hill parish.

"I'd say that qualifies. The leading man for Dean is at Trinity, Copley Square."

The sum of what I knew about Trinity Church was it was worth about twenty million, and predictably filled with prosperous liberals who were happy with how it all turned out. I recalled an exposé in the Boston Globe about its million-dollar rectory; but as invariably happens, the controversy waned to passive social acceptance. In deference to the "countless hours" the Rector selflessly devoted, the vestry explained the least the church could do was to "grant him a pedestrian commute."

"It's a celebrated church," I emptily replied, as our Scotch was arriving.

"Why is it celebrated?"

"It's—successful."

Gentry looked dubious.

"There doesn't seem to be a whole lot not to like."

"There's always something not to like," he said.

To me it was another extraneous church that provided the unintended service of guarding invaluable open space against real estate development. To this day I regret my cavalier response to Gentry's pressing question. Yet if God is the river of tributaries which I would come to believe, there are some we navigate that are bound for regret before we get to the sea.

I had already sensed Gentry's urgency before he made his request. And I had already guessed that more was at stake than his legacy as a Bishop. In deference to my gut, I couldn't help but foresee that Gentry was headed for trouble—that whatever it was, there were all the signs of a distant, gathering storm.

"There have been developments," Gentry began, "since I saw you last."

"What sort of developments?"

"The sort that can make life difficult," he replied.

"For whom?" I asked.

He pondered the question, as though he wasn't sure. Or if he was— that the question demanded an answer he didn't want to give. As the grandfather clock I passed coming in was tolling the hour of six, Gentry was roused from contemplation to explain the protocol.

"Typically, the Bishop appoints the Dean with the endorsement of the committee."

"I take it this isn't typical," I said.

"These aren't typical times. The Cathedral Warden has gotten involved—and he's no fan of mine."

"So now he's in bed with the Trustees," I said.

"You're a prophet," Gentry said.

"What will you do?"

He raised a brow. "Find the best compromise."

"I didn't know there was such a thing," I said.

"Only in an institution."

"What about in life?"

Gentry nodded: "In life, there is no such thing."

Apart from Earlie's church, the only pilgrimage I'd taken that proved to be worth the trip was half a valley down from my parents' shepherd's cottage in the foothills of the Pyrenees. Though most monasteries in the south of France had been mothballed as historical museums, Saint Férréol endured as the last active hermitage in the Vallespir. Here, faith was not a matter of abstract ideas permeated by Chanel No. 5, but brown monastic habits marinated in sweat and goat manure-vinaigrette.

At the risk of unduly romanticizing life in a monastery, I remember how mesmerized had been been by its unyielding simplicity. Three thousand miles from Victorian varnish, its gravel-strewn humility compelled me to consider a world apart from the one I had been given to live in. Far from a Puritan ethic that spawned sayings like, "weaker than religion," where I would gaze across a valley strewn with arid vineyards, and at night, sprinkled with light, I sensed in the brothers another motivation than unbridled self-congratulation—intimating something greater in this life than the illusion of personal achievement.

"There is this strange community . . ." I finally said, "that I see on Sunday night in the Old City."

"Cathedral in the Night," Gentry replied.

"Under this—cloud of light."

"Cathedral in the Night."

"It's a church?" I inquired.

He winked. "It's a cathedral."

"The guy in the leather jacket—is a priest?"

"The last time I checked," Gentry said.

"Do you know him?"

"I hired him!" Gentry laughed. "The two of you would get along! His granddad was a Bishop. And his great granddad, a Rear Admiral in the Royal Navy."

"Not exactly a chip off the old block."

"I'm not so sure," Gentry said. "When Victoria offered the Admiral knighthood for inventing a rudimentary sonar, the Admiral turned it down, explaining to the Queen that he couldn't afford the uniform."

Throwing back the last of his Scotch, Gentry glanced at his watch. "I'm wondering if you know anyone in Boston who could vouch for our prospective Dean."

I told him that I might.

"Robert Beringer," Gentry preempted my question.

"I'll ask my father."

"I'd be grateful," he said. "The stakes are getting fairly high."

# 8

FOLLOWING A THOROUGHGOING CROSS-EXAMINATION to get to the bottom of my question—"There has to be a woman!"; "Don't tell me you're religious!"; "We brought you up Episcopalian!"—my father agreed to ask around his club and let me know the scuttlebutt about Beringer and his tenure as Rector of Trinity Church, Copley Square. As I was speaking with him, I was freshly aware of the enviable hands we were in. Ben Sr. was a gifted, thoroughgoing lawyer with an extraordinary nose for bullshit.

As work was ramping up toward a business trip to Paris, after which I planned a week's vacation, I had almost forgotten my paternal request until the telephone rang. Catching up on news, my father explained that he had spoken with a fellow attorney who was a member of the vestry of Trinity Church, where Beringer was "very popular." Alluding to his talent for "raising a buck," and for "navigating the rapids," his colleague commended his "courageous stand on nuclear disarmament."

Concluding his report, Ben Sr. added: "And you asked about his work with the poor. The best I could do was that he started a homeless shelter in the Combat Zone."

"That's a long way from Copley Square," I quipped.

"Maybe longer than you think."

I submitted to the full-blown Sunday morning service in hopes of connecting with Gentry. Reluctantly yielding to the coffee hour, I endured the perfume prattle—predictably ignored by the over-sixty crowd in its quest to be "the frozen chosen." As Gentry entered, he was already engrossed in an animated conversation with a young, magnetically enchanting woman I guessed to be no more than thirty.

"Well, speak of the devil!" Gentry called, as I made my tentative approach.

"I—hope not!" I stammered.

Gentry laughed. "Ben Cabot, meet Claire McWilliams!"

"What makes you the devil?" she happily inquired.

"What doesn't?" I buried myself.

Embarrassed, I felt myself fishing for my seventh-grade list of telephone prompts. Her soft, discerning eyes, peering at the world with shy, yet unabashed amusement, gave me to believe that humility alone was the greatest feminine beauty. If her bob of chestnut hair against the fur-lined hood of her parka hadn't been enough, her generous smile, and entreating gaze, left me palpitating in the parlor.

"I've known Claire since she was a child!" Gentry said. "The McWilliams live above me on Mount Royal."

"The Bishop says the two of us are heretics!" she said.

"I can only speak for myself."

"And?" she pursued me.

I glanced at the Bishop. "I'm a heretic," I said.

"So why are you here?"

"To—talk to you!" I faltered.

Her smile forgave my clumsiness.

"I mentioned your interest in Cathedral in the Night!" Gentry interjected. Before I could head him off at the pass, he persisted: "Every Sunday at dusk!"

Watching for signs that she was feeling coerced, Claire's smile remained as generous as ever. Before I was able to still my heart, she even looked intrigued. I suggested that we meet at five o'clock in front of Christ Church Cathedral, and she gladly accepted as someone who pardoned hopeless muddlers every day.

My spacious living room proved to be too small to contain its restless occupant, and so I absconded to roam the city from Westmount east to the Village. I must have taken in every breath of longing I had ever taken in as a boy, before admitting the truth that my greatest loves of all were always in my imagination. Although I'd never understood the baffling phrase, "only in my imagination"—as if there were a love that didn't demand an imagination to receive it—as it began to snow, I was left alone to do what I did best: to imagine a horizon whose reality depended on being just beyond my reach.

Blissfully removed from the pedestrian world as I made my way through the snow, I furtively conjured a cozy chalet high in the Austrian Alps. Brooding before a crackling fire in the middle of a blinding blizzard,

I was startled by a knock on the heavy plank door that was banked by the wind and the snow. By the time I had descended the Arlberg Pass to the salt-soaked streets of Montreal, my crystalline vision of Claire McWilliams was as pure as the driven snow.

I had resolved to be stationed on the steps of the Cathedral when she arrived at five o'clock. But as I approached from Saint Catherine Street, Claire was already there. Standing in knee-high sealskin boots like an elegant Inuit, she happily acknowledged my late arrival through undulating blankets of snow.

"You need a winter coat!" she gleefully called, descending the Cathedral steps. Discreetly reviewing my overcoat, I regretted that I looked like a lawyer. Yet crossing Union Square, she put her arm through mine, spawning anthropological hopes that somewhere in the world, walking arm-in-arm was the same as being married.

As we walked down to the river, we easily exchanged abridged versions of our lives. Clearly agnostic about my vocation, she was intrigued by why I came to Montreal. In a job that demanded a cashmere coat to justify the grief in getting it, I felt strangely enveloped by an unfamiliar warmth—from someone who might care about a lawyer.

When I finally asked her what she did, Claire unassumingly explained she was a neonatal nurse in the intensive care unit of Montreal Children's Hospital. Humbled as I was by what I assumed was impossible, heartrending work, she quietly considered my impassioned questions as she gazed through the falling snow. At first I feared her silence betrayed some kind of judgment on my own narcissistic life, until I realized it wasn't in her nature—that the imagined judgment was mine.

Claire curiously asked how I met Gentry and found myself at Christ Church Cathedral. When I sheepishly confessed "social desperation," she threw back her head and laughed. As absurd as it seemed, in that fleeting moment I believed Claire McWilliams knew me.

"So, you can't say the church isn't good for something!"

"If my ambitions are for women over sixty."

Her impish grin slyly stretched to a smile, before she broke into another gale of laugher. At the risk of an impetuous declaration of love in a foreign city, I wondered if I could love another woman as much as I believed that I loved Claire. Whether "love at first sight," infatuation, or the errand of an errant fool, I knew that no matter what happened, the light in her eyes would be with me forever.

When we came upon Place d'Armes, the grand square was empty. Recalling that Cathedral in the Night was nomadic, we considered other possible venues. From a vacant Place Cartier, we walked down La Commune against the snow blowing up from the river—where, beyond the vacant firehouse on Place d'Youville, I saw a familiar glow of light.

# 9

BY THE TIME WE joined the crowd of fifty people, the service was underway. The leather-mantled priest quietly presided behind the pair of folding tables, as a communicant launched into "The Prayer of Saint Francis" from a sodden sheet of paper in the snow. I wondered if this was what the lyricist meant when he was penning "Silent Night": a mystical peace, that stills the whirling world to receive its own transcendence.

But at the end of the first line, "Lord, make me an instrument of your peace," a fight broke out from the shadows that bound the illuminated sanctuary. Before I was able to identify the source, what looked like a substantial human being hurtled through the air and landed on the table that was holding the sand-filled wooden cross. As the table collapsed, a second homeless man came careening out of the night—pouncing on his foe in apparent retribution for what sounded like a stolen sleeping bag.

Instantly between them, like a sinewy winch the priest hoisted the assailant from the pavement—holding him off as the implicated thief defeatedly got up on his own. Releasing the aggressor, he stood them side-by-side in front of the one unbroken table. Circling behind the abbreviated altar, he stared back and forth at the combatants, and as the rest of us endured the deafening silence, I thought: "Better them than me."

Then, as if nothing had happened, the priest seamlessly moved into a paradoxical reflection that made the chaotic bar room brawl look more like an orchestrated lesson. The story he retold was the famous account of "The Feeding of Five Thousand," by which he invoked an "economy of God" as opposed to the one we had just witnessed. Summoning the weary warriors into the sanctuary light, he called them each by name before undertaking a hard-boiled cross-examination.

When he asked "Matthieu" what he thought he would gain by stealing "Sebastian's" sleeping bag, both of them stood down—dead in their tracks—and soberly stared back at the priest. Invoking an afternoon several weeks before in the slums of nearby Griffintown, the priest recounted how he came upon them both, sharing a "Croque-monsieur." Concluding that the miracle of God's abundance was absolutely "économique," he asserted it was only when men give instead of take that they will ever get their fill.

It was then that he turned to the offering, which I remembered seeing at a distance. Repeating that Cathedral in the Night asked for something far more valuable than money, he admonished his scruffy congregants to offer what they had to each other. Faithfulness, hope, endurance, sobriety, loyalty, courage, strength, whispered from their lips as candles were lit from one frozen hand to the next.

One by one, homeless men came forward to the cross, visibly worse for recent wear—notably askew, yet holding enough sand to support a flickering sea of burning candles. As the illumined sanctuary drained of the flames being poured into the cruciform vessel, the priest raised his arms in the air to pronounce my nemesis: "The Peace of the Lord!" For the first time in my ritual life, I gave in to shaking hands with characters I wish I could have deployed to crash a party at the Harvard Club.

Claire vanished into the congregation, which looked more like a fraternity party. As I scanned the crowd, the sleeping bag combatants were engaged in a full-body hug—not unreminiscent of a pair of sumo wrestlers, lumbering in the snow. Watching Claire's face joyfully returning through the animated throng, it was as though the transitory light in her eyes was already beyond me.

Without missing a beat, Communion began and ended as a conversation about a man who gave his life to friends he knew were going to betray him. Blessing the meal as a sign of that life, we were invited to the intact table with the final admonition that whenever we failed, we always had the chance "to turn around." With Claire at my side, together we received a crusty chunk of a baguette, and then an earthen cup from the oily, fissured hands of a less than antiseptic acolyte.

As a hot, steaming meal was rolled out on carts at the close of Communion, the priest raised his arms in the air once again, and boldly pronounced: "The Supper!" Following Claire's lead, I braved the buffet laid out by several indigent servers, as the charismatic priest emerged from the dark to greet his unexpected dinner guests. He was striking in an enigmatic, self-possessed way, and smaller than he'd looked at the table—bearing graceful features that defied the task at hand and his rough-and-ready profession.

What I remember best were his penetrating eyes, that refined to an ironic glint. It was as if he were peering out at the world with unbounded, spontaneous amusement. "Welcome!" he said, gripping my hand, and introducing himself: "Luke Hale."

The tightly slit cut on his upper lip must have been suffered in the skirmish. As easily as Claire had slipped her arm through mine, she reached into her parka pocket, extracting a miniature first-aid kit, from which she took a square of gauze. I wondered if he felt as grateful as I felt when we were crossing Union Square, arm-in-arm; and as he pressed it to his mouth, and looked into her eyes, I could only sympathize.

I imparted to Hale that it was Bishop Gentry who had recommended the visit. Even then I gleaned something in Hale's smile that was inexplicably familiar. As obviously different as the two of them were, I sensed a commonality which I finally ascribed to the superficial fact that the two of them were priests.

I continue to wish I could have skulled the streams I didn't know connected their lives—in the same way I wish that I had been aware of the river that was carrying my own. Yet I know there was no way to foresee the turbulence awaiting us around the bend, bearing so deep and powerful a current that none of us would come back. Still, for all the uncertainty, chance and accidents that make the river what it is, I will always be grateful that there are no mistakes, save for never jumping in.

"You preach a strange economics!" I said, looking to incite the preacher.

Hale smiled. "It's a different economics," he said. "But an economics all the same."

"You said the more you give, the more you have," I said.

"I'm not the first," he replied.

"What happens when there's nothing left to give?" I came back.

"There's always something left to give."

I cast a dubious look.

"There's a difference between giving and taking," he said. "For takers, there is never enough. Most of these guys are victims of takers. They didn't get here by too much giving."

As I listened to this cocksure, renegade priest, and his subversive understanding of God, I wondered how, even with his evident gifts, he survived the institutional church.

"There's no fucking miracle in taking," he said. "The miracle is in the giving."

Claire took my cashmere arm, making me aware of the line of men waiting to see him. Thanking him for his hospitality, Claire promised that she would be back. Touching his lip, Hale tentatively smiled before turning to the lengthening line, and as I walked with Claire up Rue Saint Pierre, I already knew that I loved her.

I asked if she would like to go for a drink, and she cheerfully agreed. Though I suspected Claire wasn't one to frequent the Ritz, it was the only game in town on Sunday night. Agreeing to a glass of wine, she guessed I was inclined to higher octane—and egging me on, I finally agreed to something warmer and stronger.

"Why did you become a lawyer?" she asked, with her engaging curiosity.

"I'm not sure," I confessed. "My father was a lawyer."

She smiled, almost sympathetically.

"Not much of a reason," I apologized.

"But, a familiar one!" she said.

"Why did you go into nursing?" I asked.

"My dad is a doctor!" she laughed. "Actually, I started medical school. It almost cured me of medicine."

"Though not of nursing?"

"Not of nursing! I'm the luckiest woman in the world!"

"What did you think of Cathedral in the Night?"

"I wasn't—prepared!" she said.

"I'm not sure you could have been," I empathized.

"I mean, prepared to make sense of a church."

"Is that what it was?"

"Or whatever it was! Are we going next week?"

My heart missed a beat—before I realized I couldn't. "I'll be in France," I lamented.

"Lucky you!" she said. "Business or pleasure?"

"Actually, both," I said.

"Do you promise to come back?"

I wanted to tell her how much I didn't want to leave. Desperately in love, all I really wanted was to bask in her angelic presence. But the best I could do, taking in a smile that outshone the façade of the Ritz, was to look forward to what felt like an eternity in France in order to allow me to return.

# 10

BEFORE I LEFT AT the end of the week, I called Gentry with my father's findings. Impatient as he was with liberal politics—"Who's in favor of a nuclear explosion?"—he seemed reassured by Trinity's shelter in the red-light district of Boston. I knew what wouldn't help Gentry's impression was Ben Sr.'s concluding crack, that Beringer was said to be "very well-liked for the superlative cut of his jib."

If Paris didn't exist in the world, it would have to have been invented. Something hangs in the burnished air that presumes its preeminence, as if to suggest that nothing on earth could have stopped this incarnation. In an otherwise aimlessly random world, there was nothing random about Paris, as sightseers' eyes from Togo to Thailand bathed in its transcendent splendor.

Walking the streets in the early morning, or the freshly watered gardens at dusk, I always had the sense that Paris kept track of its every admiring subject. Wrapped in itinerant solitude, I mysteriously felt at home. Sheltered by this extroverted world, I was free to be alone.

Still, one's vision of Paris was only as great as the eyes that came to perceive it. Those who clung to American chums were lost before they had started, while those who were seized by her wandering streets knew they were only beginning. If past disappointments were brought to life by this consummate city of lights, so were the long-forgotten dreams one realized would never die.

In my vast ruminations of vaster regrets, thoughts of Claire never left me. In the Tuileries, on the Rivoli, up and down the celebrated Champs Elysees, her sweet omnipresence distracted a grief that was wrought by her heartrending absence. If absence does make the heart grow fond in men blessed by moderation, in men who are cursed by the bane of excess, it can feel like the end of the world.

So goes the way of love unrequited, whose nature is never to die. Recalling my junior semester abroad that had stretched an endless Atlantic— when my tenuous future solely depended on seven-day aerogrammes—I traded the promise of love yet to come for love that had already gone the cynical way of dismissing the past as no more than a naïve dream. And brilliant young girls, whose job it had been to plumb the depths of romance, would one day awaken to want nothing more than a house on Martha's Vineyard.

And once-kindred spirits who voraciously read and revered the Lost Generation, finally lost the nerve to be lost, and so to be found again. Fueled by the fear of what we were given to dread we would never achieve, our lives would be pimped behind decorous gates and devoured by the houses we lived in. Desperately peddling squandered hopes, we defied the humility that brings men back to their fledgling days of wisdom beyond their years.

At the end of the week I packed my valise and escaped to Gare de Lyon. Built for the World Exposition at the turn of the century—lavishly garnished in limestone detail and crowned by a lighted clock—it fronted a shed of iron and glass and Art Nouveau nostalgia that defied its idling, space-age trains aimed at the south of France. But this was before the TGV blew down to Perpignan; so, deciding to breakfast at Le Train Bleu, I awaited my rickety Pullman.

As I threaded my way through swarms of tourists into the Salle Dorée—with its Belle Époque frescos and Rococo mermaids inspiring gilt-vertigo—it was nonetheless starched with crisply dressed businessmen sipping espresso dirt, reminding the world that affluence was an international marvel. Together we fought to make rich people richer by bitterly suing each other over the value of "assets" and "instruments" that had no value at all. In good times we did well, and in bad times, better, as we fought over other men's money, until came a time when we couldn't remember why we were fighting at all.

Sometimes I pictured a pair of old bachelors on a dusty porch in Nebraska, reading the loan on the family farm had been called by an "instrument." For all the assets I may have lost, audacity wasn't one of them: beware of terms like "financial product" and hang on to your wallet. Not long ago, "products" were physical objects that could be touched—like a porch in Nebraska, which thanks to me, had been swindled from two old men.

For Theirs Is the Kingdom

I recall my fifth-year college reunion I was talked into attending. My freshman roommate, and Wall Street trader who actually worked on Wall Street, related a tale of his "talent as a teacher" when his nephew asked what he did. Fishing a penny and a quarter from his pocket, he held up the quarter to the kid, explaining he "bought these"—then holding up the penny—from other people, with "these."

There was a time when we would have been too embarrassed to admit this is what we did. But one of the rewards of our postmodern faith in the absence of true north is not having to consult a moral compass—because it wouldn't work anyway. Enviable as my success may have been to most of the working world, for the first time in my entitled life, I realized that I was lost.

Passing the railyard from Gare de Lyon on the brink of stony sleep, I thought of the women I had loved and lost, and how Claire was ineffably different. Though she wouldn't have won the pageants that were run on the stage of my professional life, nor would she have paid enough attention to know they were going on. If the impossible, romantic dreams of my past were ever fated for tomorrow, I harbored the hope the most impossible of all was somehow destined for today.

Rocked to a queasy, uneasy sleep that brought me to the south of France, I felt like a lost lover, missing in the night, who was waiting for the morning. Just above Narbonne, where the tracks began to hug the Mediterranean, I groggily wakened to the reminiscent sea, and an unexpected remnant of home. As the slender, tapered shore opened to the parched and ancient floor of the Vallespir—spreading inland from the coast like a baker's pizza peel to the foothills of the Pyrenees—it must have been a memory, lingering in some past that was waiting to fulfill its future, or some retro-causal future, drawing me back to a past that had yet to be fulfilled.

# 11

THE PERPIGNAN TRAIN STATION would have gone unnoticed if not for Salvador Dali. Declaring it "the center of the universe," little was done to fête a claim I had always imagined the egomaniacal artist must have reveled in. As I lugged my suitcase through the acrid smoke, past a bank of vending machines, there was something in its world-lost sadness that magnetically attracted me.

Roussillon was, without a doubt, the least fashionable part of southern France. Long before Fitzgerald made the Riviera famous, and Parisians were flocking to Nice, Catalan peasants three hundred miles west were plowing fields and tending sheep and vineyards. I will always be impressed that my brahman parents passed over obvious Provence, choosing to explore the romance of their youth where friends had never heard its name.

Maneuvering around the café tables that ringed the rental car garages, I left Dali's "ordinariness of God" in my extraordinary Peugeot. The slanting sun was high in the passing vineyards, now asleep in temperate winter, inspiring me to think of the uncongenial climate I was missing back home. But with the warmth of the Catalan sun on my face, I managed to get over it—saving my sympathetic regrets for a less sympathetic day.

Céret had been home to Picasso, Braque, Gris, and lesser cubist pioneers, who enjoyed the paradox of sun and shade beneath its legendary trees. Swallows raced, beak-to-tail, through the narrow streets, and long into the summer night, and I wondered if I'd see them in the winter chill, and premature dying of the light. Conjuring the village center in my mind, I decided to drive up to the house before returning for dinner and an evening to wander in the shadows of the fortified town.

Suddenly aware that it had been a decade since I'd last paid a visit, I marveled at time's passing and tried to remember what had happened in those intervening years. But as quickly I was turning on our gravel road and approaching the driveway entrance—its listing fieldstone gateposts over-grown with ronce and other lethal brands of briar. Taking on the erstwhile shepherd's path, washed out after years of disuse, I cautiously proceeded down the steep decline like a tactical military scout.

There, at the foot of the challenging descent, sat the stucco shepherd's cottage—seemingly abandoned by the owner's neglect, or shuttered by some drastic change in plan. Landing on what once had been a parking space, I exited the car, and made my way through the arbousier to the unas-suming dwelling. Even in winter, the pungent scent of thyme was heady as I rounded the house, giving me to wonder if it would have been there had I not come back again.

Standing on the terrace, I was overwhelmed anew by the sweeping panoramic view, running down the valley to a distant azure sea, span-ning twenty miles in the haze. Countless towns were scattered across the coastal floor—thatched by orchards, fields, and vineyards—and bounded on the north by the eastern Pyrenees, sprinkled with ancient castle ruins. As I stood before the shutters of the battened French doors that stretched the modest breadth of the cottage, what instantly came back was what I'd known as a boy: the unspeakable desire to fly.

Rattling the key in the iron lock, I feared what might be on the other side. When my grandmother died—having willed the house in Maine to my startlingly middle-aged mother—the more challenging logistics in-creasingly conspired to keep my parents from returning. And in the throes of law school, I probably believed I no longer had the time to come, allow-ing my parents' forty-year tradition to fade like the passing of summer.

Expecting to open the old oak door on a biology experiment, I remem-bered that our faithful Madame Vila had remained in my parents' employ. The redolent presence of verdant decay was heavy in the air—summoning the exile of lonely boyhood weeks when summer might as well have been a lifetime. It was hard to imagine my meticulous parents feeling comfortable in this space, but with the shutters flung open, and the dankness fled, I knew again the genius of this place.

There was a corner of a kitchen, and the rest of the house held a great room used in lambing season. Climbing the stairs to the pitching mez-zanine, with my suitcase banging on the railing, I traversed the bowing floor, glazed with a patina that bespoke a past of rusty tools and storage. My single bed from childhood cowered at the end, and dropping my gear to the floor, I flopped down on the mattress to sleepily absorb the centuries that had gone before.

When I started awake, the winter sun was falling behind a snow-peaked Canigou. Descending the stairs, I carted the outdoor furniture onto the terrace, and turning on the power, splashed myself awake and took my pompous Peugeot to town. As I easily parked, I realized this was not high season for sun-starved tourists, allowing a quick walk to the Grand Café, past Gauloises-smoking codgers on the street.

After a less than exceptional dinner and an exceptional bottle of wine, I over-tipped the waiter like a drunk American and angled my way out the door. The cobbled streets meandered beneath the towering trees and along the leaning parchment walls, which continued to glow in the descending dusk as if they were still clinging to the day. Save the sound of water trickling in the gutters from a canal sourced high up in the mountains, the evening hush had settled into somnolent night—grounding my imagined swallows.

A widow dressed in black was emptying a bucket in the rill that flowed beneath her door. Piquant paella, then Catalan stew, wafted from neighboring windows. Exploring "Centre-ville" in search of the Peugeot—which was amazingly found where I had left it—I felt exceedingly grateful to my faithful, underrated, if self-serious French barouche.

On the perilous way up the mountain to our shieling, either you make it or you don't. I made it—daring what I'd always fantasized as a lesser "Grande Corniche"—testing guardrail paucities which, if not respected, could land one in a hundred-meter cavern. Judiciously passing through the overgrown entrance, I muttered a prayer of thanksgiving: if not to Saint Christopher, perhaps to that celebrated martyr, "Saint Vin Ordinaire."

# 12

I DON'T REMEMBER CLIMBING the mezzanine stairs or dropping to the bed, but with the morning sun streaming through the Canigou window I felt grateful to see another day. Groping to confirm that an undersized helmet had not been squeezed onto my head, it was the first time I'd been fitted with that phantom headgear since my senior year in college. When I finally gave in to the insistent light, I agonized my way down the stairs—easing myself out onto the terrace in a windbreaker and boxer shorts.

The morning sun was clear of the Albères mountains that divided France from Spain as I sat in what was once my father's high-backed chair, and parked my feet up on the table. When the helmet had loosened enough to ascertain that it was Saturday morning, I realized I had won a fortuitous trip to the weekly outdoor market. Looking forward to filling the empty fridge with fresh fruit and vegetables, I made my descent in the added hope of an unforgiving double-espresso.

Husbands and wives in their Saturday best grazed from stall to stall throughout the town: tasting, passing judgment, critiquing, begrudgingly agreeing with a shrug of the shoulder. Husbands convened for impassioned arguments about the latest political scandal, leaving wives in peace to indignantly complain about their partners several meters away. Patronizing several Catalan vendors, I paused at a stand of cheese—where, viewing the sign, "Saint Ferréol," my curiosity was piqued.

As old as the cheese looked, the monk looked even older as he stood there in his sackcloth cassock. Irrepressibly smiling as though he'd awaited this propitious transaction all week, he ebulliently met my providential need for his solitary offering: "Brebis." Suddenly inspired to visit again the monastic haunt on the hill, I completed the purchase, and jumped in my car for that memorable promontory.

The grounds looked noticeably less maintained than I had remembered them—save a single monk looking out across the valley, the windswept mount was deserted. I parked the car on the gravel drive while the brother continued his surveillance. As I made my approach, he lurched around, and stared inquisitively.

"Bonjour!" I called.

"Bonjoo!" he called back, with a miserable French accent. "Voo nêtes pas Français!"

"Je suis Américan!"

His smile gave way to a guffaw. "By God, what brings you?" he eagerly inquired, behind an energetic approach.

"Work," I admitted, reaching out my hand, and submitting to his powerful grip.

"You sure as hell have come to the wrong place!" he laughed.

"You're not French!" I observed.

"From Rhode Island, yeah. Been here for forty years."

His inability with French was impressive.

"You sure have an eye for vistas," I observed.

"Tough to eat the scenery!" he said. Offering me a bench in the shade, he introduced himself: "Brother Joe!"

We sat down together, to take in the distant sea. "It's a beautiful place," I said.

"So, you're in real estate!" he happily remarked.

"I'm a lawyer," I confessed.

"Fine profession, yeah. And how are things back home?"

"I've been living in Canada," I said.

"An international man!" he applauded the program.

"Do you ever go back?"

Brother Joe nodded. "That's a rich man's game. No, I never have."

I thought of how my father would have said Brother Joe was "as Irish as Paddy's pig." Doing the math, he must have been sixty, but if not for his ruddy complexion he could have passed as a linebacker disguised by a premature shock of silver hair. He was one of those quiet, unassuming men one sensed had seen too much—commanding respect by a meditative silence that spoke of some hard-won wisdom.

What he did divulge was he had served in the army as an infantry "Forward Observer," and that after the Battle of Monte Cassino, landed with his comrades in Provence. Though light on military history, I remembered that legendary conflict as one of the worst and fiercest battles fought in the Second World War. In response to my query about his role, Brother Joe obliquely imparted that "FO's" guided mortar and artillery fire onto targets ahead of the front line.

As if he were grateful for this unexpected chance to retrieve something he had lost, with distant, thoughtful eyes, he spoke of coming home through the celebrated Port of New York. Describing his billet in Grand Central Station amidst "a battlefield of cots," he had listened through the night to "an ocean of breathing" of thousands of returning soldiers. With "tears of joy" for his safe return, and "tears of regret" for friends he'd lost, he described looking up at the celestial ceiling—to think that he had made it home.

After several months on the loading dock of the Railway Express in Pawtucket, young Joe O'Neill felt compelled to leave home "for some of the things that I done." Leaving it there in the virile silence, it was clear he had nothing more to say. As naive as I was about the gruesomeness of war, ballooning my gut on the moment, I nonetheless gleaned some visceral hope that must have brought him to this day.

"And in my wanderings, I found this place!" Joe jolted us back to the present. "'Course now we'se just a bunch of old coots! All eleven of us!"

When the monastery's Bishop closed the hermitage "for lack of adequate resources," the eleven monks decided to go it on their own as "self-declared Roaming Catholics! The truth is," Joe went on, "the kitchen was costin' the Bishop too damn many francs! But hell," he puzzled, shaking his head, "everybody needs to eat!"

A Deux Chevaux bounced up the dusty drive and came to an uneasy rest. I guessed it was arriving from the Saturday market when the octogenarian sprang loose, and attempted to untie a familiar-looking sign lashed to the canvas roof. Brother Joe jumped up, winking to inform me he would have to take care of this himself—offering his hand, if not the certainty that I hadn't seen the last of him.

"I'm Ben," I belatedly introduced myself.

"Ben, I'll remember ya'!" he said. "And when you gets back home, remember that we all's make one damn fine dinna'!"

"I look forward to it."

"Good!" he said—to say the deal was done. As he turned and headed down toward the aged monk, he waved over his shoulder: "One damn fine dinna'!" he cheerfully called. "And one helluva good bottle of wine!"

# 13

FOR THE MYRIAD TIMES I have gone away for business or for pleasure, I am always surprised that the home I left somehow survived in my absence. If thawing banks of snow and salt-soaked streets meant spring to Montreal, its lingering gray seemed far away from the sun-drenched fields of Céret. Still, passing the Ritz in search of a trace of the woman I had left in the snow, gave rise to the hope that the ice-bound ground might yet give way to a flower.

Thanks to the six-hour time advantage, I was up at the crack of dawn. For all the uncertainties I had left, I was anxious to see Gentry again. And despite what I knew were formidable odds that Claire would be sitting in a pew, as I timidly approached the Cathedral steps, my gut churned like an adolescent's.

Surveying the graying congregation, I confirmed that the odds were none. Though the chances were good that Gentry would be out conducting parish visits, I nonetheless had a premonition that I would find him in the Bishop's chair. Glad to see his reassuring face, albeit in a miter at a distance, I managed to endure the Lenten penitential pomp to greet him in the narthex.

"I thought you'd left us!" Gentry exclaimed. "It's been almost a month!"

I was flattered he had noticed.

"Are you free for brunch?"

I told him that I was.

"Wonderful!" he said, shaking my hand. "I'll see you at the Ritz at noon!"

It would be difficult for any hotel named the Ritz to escape being satirized, but if any one could, I suspect it would be the Ritz-Carlton of Montreal. Having survived several economic quakes over its hundred-year life, it endured as the oldest hotel by the name in North America. Elegantly frayed like a gilded garment at the heart of the Golden Mile, its white-gloved presence on Sherbrooke Street was proof of how it was meant to be.

As I entered the lobby, the Bishop was standing on the steps of the erstwhile ballroom, speaking with several men I surmised were Westmount Anglicans. Respecting what looked to be a burdened conversation, I waited out the exchange. But noting my arrival, he launched into a round of presti-digital farewells; then, as if out in a field, he waved me over and athletically leapt up the stairs.

"How was France?" he called, as I pursued my host.

"What's not to like!" I called back. "How was Montreal?"

I heard him chuckle. "Not as much to like," he said.

From my side of the table, Gentry looked tired, and perhaps a little bit older. I offered a review of the virtues of Paris before taking him south on the train. Once he was delivered to the Vallespir, his countenance instantly changed—as though he had just fought through irritating tourists to the only thing that mattered.

"Are you far from the Tech?"

"Less than an hour into the mountains," I said.

"I hear it's a hell of a trout river," he said.

"Consider yourself invited."

He looked back, unconvinced.

"I mean it," I said.

He smiled. "I look forward to it."

"What's happening here?" I cut to the chase.

"What the hell isn't?" he said. "The committee plans to have the new Dean in place in a matter of months."

"Who's the favorite?"

"I wouldn't know. They're keeping it to themselves."

"How is that?" I asked.

Gentry shrugged. "I'm out."

"What do you mean, you're 'out'?"

"I'm out," he repeated.

"How could you be 'out'? You're the Bishop!" I protested.

"The same way I got in."

"How did you get in?"

"The church is a club," Gentry said. "He who lives by the club dies by the club. It's just blunter than the sword."

"Who knows," I said, "the new Dean may surprise you."

"I'd wager your man from Boston."

"Why is that?" I asked him.

"No one speaks as well 'on the other hand.'"

I laughed. "What happened to the first hand?" I asked.

"It's called the truth," he said.

"Which is never very good for the health," I granted.

"It wasn't good for Christ's," Gentry said.

"So much for his career in the church."

"He would have made a lousy Dean."

The Bishop devoted the rest of brunch to angling in Roussillon: an episcopal piscine cross-examination for which I had few answers. When he glanced at his vintage Hamilton watch squaring off toward two, I braved the subject I had harbored for a month—if not for a romantic lifetime. "Claire McWilliams," I timidly began.

"I just spoke with her dad!" Gentry said.

My heart began to palpitate.

"Claire moved to the Old City!"

"Claire?" I helplessly floundered.

"Though, the good Doctor isn't happy!" he declared. "Another thing for which I'm being blamed!"

Oblivious to my implosion of grief, Gentry pleasantly rolled on: "When John McWilliams went to the Medical School, the hospital lost a great surgeon. But when Claire decided to become a nurse, we lost a fine physician!"

As lethal a blow as it already was, I hung on Gentry's every word. "She always had a way of getting his goat—from the time she was a little girl! Claire is exactly like the old man! Now, he can't blame me for that!"

"What does he blame you for?"

"For working with Luke!" Gentry indignantly decried.

I sat there, feverish.

"He says that Cathedral in the Night was my idea!"

Explaining that I wasn't feeling well, I scanned the ballroom for an "Exit" sign. Gentry's concern for my overwrought reaction had me feeling embarrassed. But thanking him profusely, I purposefully departed—with absolutely no place to go.

The pummeled van was parked before the Bank of Montreal in the twilight of the late afternoon, as two spectral figures across the ghostly square were building a cathedral of light. Avoiding detection, I circled

Place d'Armes in the sweetness of the thawing winter air, and it began to snow when a figure, then another, traipsed across the plaza. The minute hand was falling from the top of the clock as familiar silhouettes approached the table—coming to rest in the ephemeral light like an inadvertent living crèche.

I looked again for Claire, and then for Hale. I had lost track of both of them. Watching the worshipers streaming from the shadows to that eerily welcoming light, I held fast to the vision as I wistfully passed into the vast and solitary night.

# 14

IF I WERE A genuine victim of betrayal, I could also have been a martyr. The fact is, the closest I had ever come to an authentic scrape with injustice was that which, in the name of the rule of law, I managed to perpetrate on others. Stretched between playing the honorable man who had never intended to lie—and an unconscious swindler who suddenly awakes to the unfortunate truth too late—I went about those ensuing days lamenting a bankrupt past, in the growing realization I had little to show for an already ransomed future.

The ring of my phone was about as frequent as the bleep of my smoke alarm. The social life I thankfully left in the revelrous streets of Boston was dramatically reduced to telephone tag with middle-aged secretaries. So, when the telephone abruptly interrupted one of my late-night soup extravaganzas, my heart leapt with the hope that in spite of the hour, it could only be Claire.

As I listened to her fresh, salvific voice splashing from the other end, I gave up my abstinence like Lent in hopes of an early Easter. Like a keen cryptographer, I deciphered her tone for the slightest note of affection. She welcomed me home, inquired about France, then shyly requested "a favor"—inspiring me to detect how a "favor" could be code for my hand in marriage.

When she asked me when we would be able to meet, I blurted out, "How about now?" She laughed, then suggested a greasy spoon in the depths of Rue Sainte-Antoine—explaining that "Luke might be able to come," accompanied by an "Henri." As inscrutable as the mission remained, and as stumped as I was by "Henri," I was able to devise a rationale for why Hale was just along for the ride.

The joint was clad in iron bars, and steeped in roll-your-own smoke. Braving the noxious humidor, Claire eagerly waved from the back. Next to her sat a diminutive man—and Quebecois if there was one—offering me a toothless smile as Hale offered me a chair.

There was something ancient about his face, though I couldn't discern what it was. His leathery skin was creased in the way of an indigenous tribal chieftain. Behind two weeks' growth of what I guessed was prematurely graying stubble, he looked me in the eye as if he knew something important I had yet to know.

Fearing I'd been billed as some kind of savior, I hoped that the "favor" was legal. I shook Hale's hand and smiled at Claire with unconvincing aloofness—before Henri sprang up, and offered his own with an expectant twinkle in his eye. By his wide-eyed countenance I rightly concluded that Henri spoke little English, before Claire embarked on what I would learn was an all too common tale of woe.

As sous-chef of one of the best continental restaurants in Montreal, Henri was at the top of his game when his wife confessed her affair. Wanting to avert a family insurrection, Henri gave her the house and moved into a nearby apartment to father his three young children. When he began to drink, he lost his job, and finally the apartment—and too proud to reside in a homeless shelter, decided to live on the street.

As I watched Hale admiring Claire's impassioned account of Henri's luckless fate, I recalled the first time I happened on him, with Claire's arm threaded through mine. To be honest, I felt like the lovesick lad who endured an interminable weekend, only to find at the Monday morning bell that he had lost everything he'd thought he had. It was eminently clear that it was different now: that at some point while I was gone, the two of them became physically relaxed—in the way of intimates.

I might have taken cover under the table, if not for the suspected wads of gum. Rather than surrendering to histrionics, or lunging for a cigarette, I politely deferred to the budding romance as one who couldn't be happier. Since I didn't smoke—or engage in the practice of running outdoors to scream—I successfully contained my adolescent anguish to listen to the rest of the story.

Fervently agreeing whenever Claire lighted on nouns like "job," or "house," Henri cracked his knuckles as though he couldn't have said it any better. Claire tactfully explained that Henri was drinking most of the time he was homeless, but now six months sober, was ready to take on the responsibilities of an apartment. Otherwise qualified for public housing, due to his delinquency he faced a two-year wait unless there was a way to appeal his case in court.

As an international finance lawyer in a domestic housing case, I felt like a Medievalist queried about quarks because he was an academic. Excusing myself as a rarefied attorney who was of little practical value, I told them I could speak to a colleague in the firm who did real estate work for the city. Henri looked disarmingly excited—as though the case had been settled—and meeting Claire's eyes across the smoky table, I feared that she believed it too.

Hale asked if I would stay for a bite. As a man who enjoyed a greasy burger as much as anyone, the truth is I had lost my appetite—along with my romantic future. If I had fallen prey to the American illusion that anything was possible, for the first time in my entitled life I suspected that it wasn't true.

Hale handed over the documents which he had organized in a folder. In that moment, what frustrated me most was that it was nobody's fault. By God, or chance, or relentless evolution, the future I'd designed was changing—and if change was an inevitable sign of life, so was the collateral damage.

On returning home, I sat by the fire in the living room with the file. Except for its unravelling lifeline to Claire, the case was uncomplicated. Evicted for nonpayment of six months' rent, Henri was out in the cold.

Were it not for Claire I probably would have dropped the file in the fireplace. Although Henri had a case, it would have taken months, or years, to get a hearing. But in reality, this "philanthropic" work was devoid of philanthropy—and replete with the self-interest of a longing heart that didn't know what it was longing for.

# 15

THE NEXT DAY I caught up with a partner in the firm who was born in Montreal: an amicable colleague from whom I thought I might be able to extract a favor. A natural baritone, or heavy smoker—in retrospect, probably both—Maurice was a well-dressed Quebecois with significant political connections. Following my convoluted appeal that posed more questions than it answered, he scanned the documents while standing in the hall and said he would get back to me.

"Say, Ben!" he called from his office door, through a magnificently porcelain smile. "Did a woman get you into this?"

"What do you think?"

He laughed. "Yes and no!"

"Then yes and no it is!"

Maurice winked. "It's the yes you need to worry about."

The next afternoon I received a call that Maurice wanted to see me. His assistant showed me to the corner office, where he was talking on the telephone—leaning back in his executive chair, working out something almost legal. He motioned me to sit, then pushed an envelope across his expansive desk before winding up the call with an enthusiastic burst that foretold the conversation's end.

Hanging up the phone, he cavalierly nodded at the legal-sized envelope. I thanked him in advance, anticipating a dubious explanation. But he wanted to know how I'd gotten involved in this "unlikely scenario," giving rise to an account of Cathedral in the Night and my ambiguous relationship to Claire.

Poker-faced, Maurice peered at me—as one who knew me better than I'd thought. "Somehow you don't seem like an American," he said.

"I'm a Canadian," I said.

"I thought you were an American!"

"I'm a dual-national."

"Jesus Christ!" he barked. "You're a half-American—who lives in Canada! You speak French—but on the English side of town! You're a corporate lawyer—who works for the poor!"

"And I go to church, but don't believe in God."

Bearing down on me, he unexpectedly asked, "What the hell do you believe in?"

I was taken aback. In an office like mine, it was not the sort of question a colleague was inclined to ask. If college was our chance to consider "beliefs" on the longest horizons of our lives—flinging shoes, footballs, and the Marx and Engels Reader at our vilest philosophical opponents—by the time I got to law school, and was buckling under the weight of Constitutional Law, there was little time to entertain beliefs beyond how best to make a living.

"I'm not sure I believe in anything," I said—as unsettling as it was for me to hear. "What do you believe in?"

Maurice looked stumped. "Family. Family, and friends."

"Do you have friends?" I asked him.

"I have family!"

"That wasn't my question," I said. "I asked if you had friends."

Averting his eyes, Maurice grinned. "No," he said.

"Do you go to church?"

"Of course not!" he retorted.

"Why not?"

"Because I believe in God!"

I laughed. "So, it's one or the other?" I said.

"Why don't you believe in God?" he asked.

"I didn't say I didn't."

He looked unconvinced.

"What difference does it make?" I said.

He nodded at the envelope. "Ask your friend," he said. "Ask your friend if he believes in God."

As a formidable partner who was known in the firm as a force to be reckoned with, the last case I imagined seeing him appeal would have been the case for God.

"I'll bet he does," he said.

"How do you know?"

"Haven't you—what's the word for 'quêter'?"

"Panhandle," I told him.

"Don't you ever talk to those guys up on Sainte Catherine Street?"

"You do?" I inquired.

"Once the loonie's in the cup, the conversation always turns to God."

"How often?" I asked.

"How often what?" he said.

"How often do you have these conversations?"

He laughed. "All the time! Jesus Christ, don't you?"

I felt oddly disconcerted.

"And you probably think they're lazy!" he prodded.

"What do you think?" I asked.

Maurice winked. "The street is hard work. And I know a lot of lazy lawyers."

Pondering these unpredicted insights from an otherwise predictable attorney, I wondered what enabled him to walk through this wall that had imprisoned my privileged life. I even wondered if, as a kid, Maurice might have been a "Protector of the Animals"—and if somewhere down the line, together we'd forgotten that the world was for everyone. Just as I was feeling like the stereotypic "Ugly American," he got up from his desk, pulled open the top drawer, and plucked something out of the tray.

Coming over to my chair, he motioned me to stand. "You may be a Canadian," Maurice declared, "but that doesn't make you a Quebecois!" With that, he pinned a small Provincial flag into the lapel of my suit, declaring me an honorary citizen of a place that almost felt like home.

Taking the envelope, I thanked him again—pausing at his office door. "Why do you think," I curiously asked, "these conversations always turn to God?"

Without missing a beat, Maurice replied, "Because the only God they know was poor!"

"So, where does that leave us?" I anxiously came back.

Maurice smiled. "With no friends."

I left my house on Sunday at dusk with the envelope inside my jacket. When I arrived on Place d'Armes, the somber city square was as cold as the apocryphal freezer. Claire was in a shiver, standing next to Hale, who was welcoming the crowd to "God's Table"—and as I watched her face, beaming in the night, it was almost too much to bear.

Wishing it were simply a matter of a lover I realized I would never have, I was suddenly faced with the consummate expression of the man

I would never be. There was something in the spontaneous way that Hale regaled the Last Supper which gave me to believe I was the lesser man, and to fear that I would always be. Yet, unlike jealous men, who are given to inspire jealousy in other men, he somehow overwhelmed the fourth deadly sin by the power of generosity.

As Hale raised his hands in the winter air before the pantheonic Bank of Montreal, there was something that united this strange community of which I was no longer a part. It was not that I believed I had been excluded, but that I had excluded myself—from some paradoxical way of the world that defied everything I had been taught. As if telepathic, at the Benediction Hale looked up through the milling throng, and after a cacophonous, final "Amen!" called to me, "Any luck?"

I crossed into the light and handed him the document promising Henri's lease. He scanned the cover letter. "You have to tell Henri."

"You tell him," I replied.

"Then you tell Claire," he said.

"I have to go," I said.

"So, this is no big deal," he came back.

"It's nothing," I dismissed it.

"Maybe not to you. It sure as hell is something to Henri."

Before I could mount a credible defense, I realized I was guilty as charged.

"I'm sorry," I said.

He smiled, and raised a brow like a forgiving older brother. "It isn't your fault. It's nobody's fault. It's only ours to fix it."

# 16

WHEN I TOLD HALE the lease would be ready on Monday, he suggested that we meet at the Cathedral. The diocesan offices were noticeably quiet when I arrived at five o'clock; an unmanned reception desk allowed me liberal passage to Gentry's door, angled in light. Coming upon the ominous rumble of a ponderous conversation, I saw a pair of field boots extending from a chair, reflecting a lapping fire.

"Just the man we were talking about!" Gentry greeted me. Rising from his chair, he came over to the door and received me into his office. I had suspected the field boots belonged to Hale, who immediately got up as Gentry retreated to a yew wood sideboard laden with crystal decanters.

"The man or the lawyer?" I belatedly retorted.

"There's a difference?" Gentry said.

"If there isn't, I'm in trouble."

Gentry laughed. "If there isn't, we're all in trouble!"

Hale retrieved another chair and set it in front of the fire. Steering a sparkling trio of tumblers into their rightful hands, Gentry raised his glass and toasted what he called, "This unlikely trinity!" We sat down together in a virile silence befitting the old-world office, as Gentry's single barrel seared our sinuses with seaweed, spices, and old rope.

"I like your boots," I said.

"Thanks," Hale said, scrutinizing his feet.

"You had those in the Amazon," Gentry remarked.

"They weren't issuing these in Vietnam."

"You served in Vietnam?" I asked.

"As a medic, yeah."

"I didn't know you were American," I said.

"Funny you should ask!" Gentry bantered.

Hale smiled. "I'm not," he said.

I probably looked puzzled.

"Back then all it took was a post office box in Detroit."

"So, how did you get to the Amazon?" I asked.

Gentry was enjoying himself.

"I was in the Mekong Delta. I guess it felt like home."

"And I poached him from the jungle!" Gentry said.

From what I could surmise, Gentry met Hale on a hunting expedition in Brazil. Hale was a guide, and an apprentice to a shaman, before leaving his Secoya tribe. With paternalistic pride, Gentry entertained us with a host of Amazonian adventures—to which Hale responded that his "favorite Bishop" was "suffering serious delusions."

"If the three of us were thrown out of a plane over any jungle in the world, only one of us would be sure to make it out, and it wouldn't be you or I!"

"Jungles aren't the problem," Hale came back.

Gentry winked. "It's churches."

"Anyway, what would be the point?" Hale mused.

"What would be point of what?" I asked.

"Of coming out alone," Gentry imparted. "I'm afraid with Luke, it's all or nothing."

As intrigued as I was by any personality that clearly outstripped my own, I was still more intrigued by what in God's name had inspired Hale to become a priest. The short version was that he read for Holy Orders in lieu of seminary, and under Gentry's mentorship, developed the plan for Cathedral in the Night. I was going to ask about his family past to which Gentry once alluded, when Gentry deftly steered the conversation back to Hale's ministry.

"Is Cathedral in the Night a church?" I asked.

"I don't think of it that way," he said.

"What is it?" I pursued him.

He considered the question. "For me . . . it's a practice," he said.

"A contemplative practice?"

"You could call it that."

"What would you call it?" I pressed.

"I'm not sure I'd call it anything," Hale said. "It's a lot more interesting to do it."

"Do you meditate?" I impulsively inquired.

Gentry laughed: "Has he ever stopped?"

"So, Cathedral in the Night is nothing new," I said.

"Nothing new," Hale said.

"The most significant difference between Cathedral in the Night and Christ's ministry," Gentry said, "is that unlike our Lord's, Father Hale enjoys the distinct advantage of a truck."

"No," Hale came back, "the most significant difference is that he chose a temperate climate."

"You wouldn't go inside if you could!" Gentry said.

Hale may have conceded the point.

"Why not?" I asked him.

He shrugged his shoulders. "When you're inside, others are left out."

"And when you're outside—everyone is in?"

Hale barely nodded.

"Everyone?" I asked, glancing at his Bishop.

"Everyone," Hale said.

"You see what I'm up against?" Gentry groused, relishing the heresy.

"So, what do you make of Jesus's claim that no one comes to God but by him?"

"What's the problem?" Hale came back.

His confidence should have rankled me.

"How can there be a single way?" I protested.

"When the way is including everyone."

It seemed like a trick answer.

"Christ's problem with the Pharisees had nothing to do with their tradition. Some scholars think he was a Pharisee. His problem with the Pharisees was that they excluded the people they were called to include."

"Which people?" I pursued him.

"The poor. The refugees. The people who are still excluded."

"So much for middle-class Christianity," I said, looking back at Gentry.

"Jesus wasn't the first Christian," Hale said. "Jesus was the ultimate Jew."

I must have looked perplexed.

"The genius of Jesus wasn't that he founded Christianity. The genius of Jesus was revealing to the world that Judaism was for everyone."

"I don't suppose you'd like to hear Luke's solution to Christ being God's only son!"

"To be honest," I said, looking back at Hale, "that's my second least favorite claim."

"May I?" Gentry said, goading his priest.

Hale blithely shrugged his shoulders.

"According to Luke, the church has made 'Christ' into Jesus's last name."

I practically guffawed: "I didn't know he had one!"

"It's Joseph-son," Hale said.

As the laughter was subsiding, Hale easily went on, "'Christ' means 'the anointed one.' According to the Scriptures we can all be anointed. Stephen the Christ, Henri the Christ, Claire the Christ," Hale said. "Hell, Ben—even Ben the Christ!"

"And how can four of us . . . be one 'Anointed One'?"

"Jesus Christ, Ben—when we're one!"

I cast my dubious look.

"You're no good at economics! You're no good at math! Thank God you're a helluva lawyer!"

Despite my disregard for religious doctrine, as the hilarity abated, I began to feel increasingly unsettled by Hale's iconoclastic convictions. It was not that I didn't resonate with his radically inclusive spirit. It was rather that, however far we may have come from burning heretics at the stake, even in this time of the church's decline, his convictions seemed dangerous.

It was seven o'clock when I reached for my case and grabbed the offer to lease. Handing it to Hale, he drew out a knife and slit open the envelope. When he saw the sheaf of bills clipped to the lease, he balked: "What the hell is this?"

"Subsidized rent is still rent," I said.

I was afraid he wouldn't take it.

"I wanted to buy him some time," I said.

He looked at me. "Thanks," he said.

"And now for something Luke will not be thankful for," Gentry interjected. "The Dean-elect is scheduled to be in town next week, and you're both invited to dinner!" Describing it as Beringer's "formal introduction to the Cathedral powers-that-be," he added, "and of course to ensure the parsonage is suitable to his wife."

When I said I could make the Thursday evening date, Gentry grinned at his priest.

"Bishop," Hale very dryly replied, "I'm afraid I have to decline."

"In case you haven't noticed," Gentry turned to me, "Luke is allergic to clergy."

"Have you met the Dean-elect?" I curiously asked.

"Yes and no," Hale answered.

"No," Gentry clarified Hale's reply, "the two have never met."

"So how could it be 'yes'?"

Hale artfully smiled. "I suspect we've met a hundred times."

# 17

ARRIVING AT THE MANSE on McGregor Avenue, I was greeted by a man at the door who perfunctorily took my coat and scarf and led me across the entry floor. As I came into the living room the Bishop was engrossed in a lively conversation with a handsome, youthful cleric in a starched white linen collar and impeccably tailored pinstripe suit. Gentry looked at ease as I made my approach, but before he could launch an introduction, the priest charged ahead, offering his hand like an energetic prep school referee.

"Ben!" he exclaimed, taking me aback by his unexpected knowledge of my name. "I'm Rob. Rob Beringer!" he liberally offered. His convincing humility instantly compelled me to trust his best intentions—if not to feel grateful that he'd gone to the trouble to discover who I was.

Harbinger of Hollywood and corporate success, his definitively angular jaw belied an authority that justified the pride to which he was clearly entitled. His inquisitive eyebrows were perpetually arched—as if affixed to some provocative question—allowing his expression to span the spectrum between assertiveness and magnanimity. There was an ambient kindness in his boyish demeanor that would have shamed the most hard-nosed skeptic; and shaking his hand, I knew why he had been the unanimous choice of the committee.

Nothing in his manner indicated less than a disarmingly compassionate priest who had gotten in the way of an embarrassment of riches from an otherwise fair-handed God. He comported his advantage with a sheer magnificence that must have been his colleagues' envy—yet countered by a self-effacing gratitude that made me want to be his friend. Before I could express my sense of debt to this newfound compatriot, the butler from the foyer arrived at my arm with a sixteen-year Lagavulin.

"We were discussing the difference between Canadians and Yanks!" Gentry roundly pronounced.

"And what was your conclusion?"

Gentry laughed. "That one is no worse than the other!"

"Or better," I retorted.

"Come now, Ben!" he said. "That's downright un-American!"

"You're a Harvard man!" Beringer said, on the verge of a non sequitur. "When did you graduate?"

I confessed the year.

"Then you must have known Charlie Abercrombie!"

I did know Charlie. "Wasn't he a rower?"

"Don't tell me you crewed with Charlie!"

Fearing athletic exaggeration, I retreated to understatement: "The day I managed to get into Harvard was the day they axed the swimming test."

If Beringer considered that he may have overplayed my value as a Boston Cabot, his unassuming smile successfully masked the need for recalibration. He went on to explain how his years at Williams—"Happy as they were"—had in retrospect, ultimately proved "lamentably elitist." Impressed by this egalitarian spirit, I found myself intrigued that despite his favorable circumstance, he was able to critique his own good fortune.

Indeed, there was something in Beringer's demeanor that felt almost familiar. Not that I was any match for his good looks, but there was something in his optimism that suggested a common tribal aspiration that was ours to celebrate together. Maybe it was his modesty that moved me to believe in his goodwill—a goodwill confirmed by his formidable wife, who stormed in from the powder room.

"How are you, Ben?" she introduced herself. "You didn't think I'd stay at home! This one," she went on, with a passing hitchhike thrown in her husband's general direction, "wouldn't look after the needs of his wife if he had all the money in China!"

I sensed there had been prior discussion concerning the Dean's residence, and that after some financial negotiation, a gentleman's agreement was reached. Yet I suspected that Sally's consternation had less to do with the house than with a natural aggression likely developed on a field hockey pitch at Choate. If, as my father liked to say, she was one of those women who was able to "talk on the inhale," I had to admire her patent disregard for the Victorian rules of the room.

On the other hand, and other end of the table, sat Gentry's understated spouse. By her silver-haired elegance I wondered if she felt the role of Bishop's wife was beneath her. To the extent that Gentry came from economic means, it appeared that so had Mrs. Gentry—suggesting she had other social fish to fry which had little to do with her husband.

"So, what is there to do in Montreal?" Sally unabashedly erupted.

The table was clearly unprepared for the question—save perhaps her husband.

"What is there to do in Boston?" Beringer attempted a rescue.

"Plenty!" she came back. "Rob, we're in Canada! This is another country!"

When I declared Montreal the most romantic city in North America, Sally replied with astonishment: "And Ben—you're from Boston!"

"Your work with the poor," Gentry interceded, "is it central to Trinity's mission?"

Beringer thoughtfully deliberated. "The poor are at the heart of everything we do. After all, Jesus was homeless."

"Really?" Sally asked. "Then why is the shelter three miles away from the church?"

"That's where the homeless are."

"Rob, they're everywhere! Even in Copley Square!"

Beringer sighed, with visible regret: "The poor will always be with us."

This was another of Jesus's sayings that bothered the hell out of me. It was not that I didn't believe it was true. It was rather that it seemed like a convenient excuse for not doing something about it—for accepting poverty as the way of the world, if not as the will of God.

"I assume he didn't mean for us to give up."

Beringer looked relieved. "Thank you, Ben," he said. "It has to be one of the most misread verses in the Gospels."

"And how do you read it?"

He graced me with his gaze. "That in the end . . . all of us are poor."

"Though some of us are poorer than others," Gentry said.

Beringer laughed. "Touché!"

With the arrival of dessert, Gentry cast a line in a not unpredicted direction, asking Beringer how he felt about "sacred real estate." I suspected that following his interviews, Beringer was well aware that there might be treacherous fishing ahead, and he would have to be careful what he fished for. Adeptly avoiding a direct confrontation about "the destruction project," Gentry delivered a false cast above the water to bait what could be lurking beneath.

Beringer willingly rose to the surface, in deference to the fisherman. Cautiously nibbling long enough to sense there might be a hook in the hackle, he "regretted the unfortunate experience of Saint Bartholomew's in New York." Having sold its air rights, which were "given by God," it "forsook its mission to the poor"—inspiring him to express his relief that he hadn't gotten "the job."

I detected a furtive kick from Sally underneath the table. It appeared that the Bordeaux was having its elegant way with the Dean-elect. Unable to discern if he regretted the remark or the undoubted contusion on his shin, I was nonetheless impressed by the aplomb with which he wrapped it up: "What a joy to be here!"

If that inaugural dinner now seems fatefully clear, it is clear only in retrospect. As I put on my overcoat in the hall, I concluded that I liked Beringer. Before leaving the two of them in front of the Ritz, I remember feeling genuinely happy when Beringer promised that once they'd gotten settled, he would be sure to give me a call.

# 18

IF DENIAL IS A river in Egypt, I spent the spring searching for the river. Whether I was smitten by love or love's absence, I missed her like a wistful adolescent. But hearing Ben Sr.'s paternal admonition to get up and dust off my britches—while sensing my mother's sympathy on behalf of her son's romantic future—I stooped to a level of desperation I never would have imagined, subjecting myself to the alumna network in search of an eligible partner.

The first was a Wellesley graduate, who had earned her degree honestly. When I discovered she had hunted down my Beacon Hill address and Law Review in a single sniff, I found myself wishing I had gotten the check before the paté arrived. And the last, whose interest in the question of God was "the summit of her life," glimpsed the financial implications of my own, and almost fell asleep in her soup.

It was early August when I got the call from the new Cathedral Dean. Hearing that he was happily ensconced in the renovated "Deanery," I guessed the lull of summer allowed him to pursue truant parishioners like me. Sally was in Boston, winding up her job as "a headhunter for CEO's"— an occupation for which I had no doubt she was ideally suited.

Beringer gladly accepted my offer to take him out to dinner. Suggesting several lesser known bistros sprinkled around the city, he settled on the Ritz because, as he said, it was "in the neighborhood." I met him at seven under the marquee and first proposed a drink at the bar—immediately sensing his ebullient spirit had to do with fleeting bachelorhood.

As often as I'd envied married friends who went home to their families, I have always been surprised by their childlike excitement at being out on the town. As the Dean took down his Scotch, I thought he might as well be drinking testosterone. Yet his self-effacing charm—stopping credibly short of being obsequious—convinced me that Beringer already knew he had won a faithful confidante.

"Where did you prep?" the Dean inquired.

"I didn't."

"You went to public high school?"

"I went to Boston Latin."

He looked reassured. "That's as good as public school gets!"

"The Bishop is thankful that you share his concern about the construction proposal."

"I'm lucky to have Stephen as my Bishop," he said.

"He's a good man—and it seems a good Bishop."

"It's a difficult job," Beringer allowed. "I mean, who would want to be a Bishop?"

"I take it, not you."

"There's no better job than being a Cathedral Dean!"

As one who felt increasingly at odds with his job, I have to say I envied him. I tried to imagine what it would be like to find my fulfillment before forty. At the risk of trying our untried friendship, if not my naive optimism, I enthused about his happy dilemma: "So, where do you go from here?"

"I've barely gotten started!" he suddenly snapped. "Are you trying to get rid of me?"

Seeing that I was taken aback, awkwardly, Beringer laughed. "Forgive me," he repented, "it has been a long day! With I suspect, many more to come!"

I told him not to worry, and suggested we make good on our waiting reservation. Jumping at the chance, he looked eager to avail himself of an intermission. As I watched him admiring the dining room, I was glad I had brought him to the Ritz—guessing that in his new position as Dean he would be able to use it well.

In retrospect, my uncharacteristic decision not to have a second Scotch may have been a sign that in spite of our detente, I didn't entirely trust him. Yet, sympathetic as I was with his being a priest, and perhaps with being Sally's husband, I liberally allowed him my share of the wine, which he impressively consumed. Well-oiled as he was by dinner's end, he applauded my own "vocation," waxing eloquent about "the practice of the law in the eternal service of God!

"Which is why I keep thinking of 'The Mammon Plan,'" he said, parking an elbow on the table. "I mean—I get Steve's concern. But wouldn't four million a year insure God's reign on earth?"

In spite of the Dean's marinated view, it nonetheless made sense to me. If Christ Church Cathedral's mission to the poor could be sustained by the rich, then why not harvest the auspicious fruits of private free enterprise? So, awash as I was in Beringer's Burgundy vision of "The City of God," I left him on Sherbrooke, an appreciative guest, if not an adoptive brother.

For the rest of the summer I forgot the church with the rest of my generation. Following the single service I attended, I failed to get Beringer's attention, engrossed as he was in a conversation with what looked to be the Senior Warden. When he indifferently waved—or waved me off—I wondered if I'd misconstrued his plea to "forgive" him for what I had taken as a genuine apology.

Suspecting that Gentry was at his fishing camp on the Miramichi River, I guessed the Bishop's absence was generously timed for Beringer's benefit. It wouldn't be unlike Gentry to fall on the sword for a greater cause—in this case, allowing his subordinate to take the reins on his own. In any event, as I sat in my pew with one foot out the door, I concluded that whatever "long days" were ahead, Beringer was up to them.

Sermonic allusions to popular culture enlivened the congregation, precipitating ripples of decorous laughter that surprised even the English. Beringer's admission to his "anger at God" for an injury braved at Saint Paul's, had his faithful flock mourning the Dean's would-have-been football career. If I had to agree with my father's contention that charm is a form of deceit, I continued to believe that Beringer escaped such motives of lesser men.

The Sunday after Labor Day bore the seasonal signs of a new beginning. The pews were replenished with well-pressed Anglicans and equally turned-out children, as Sunday school, adult education programs, and Cathedral committees were announced. Though Gentry looked bronzed in the Bishop's chair—a vestige of the summer gone—as he gazed into space, I wondered why it was that he appeared so drawn.

It was then that I glanced at the bulletin and noted in bold italics: "The Committee to Discern the Cathedral's Future for the Twenty-first Century." The evasive verbiage should have tipped me off before the Senior Warden stood up. Turning around in his family pew, he announced the Vestry's decision to "review anew the construction proposal in the light of a sustainable future!"

Looking back to the Bishop's chair, its solemn occupant sat motionless in his purple cassock, staring implacably ahead. I had never seen Gentry look vulnerable. Watching him recess behind a sea of acolytes, deacons, and portly priests, I suspected that during his August absence, Gentry had been outmaneuvered.

I phoned the next day, and was told by his assistant that the Bishop wasn't taking calls. When I left my name, she sounded unimpressed. As I considered braving the Bishop's residence in spite of the torrential rain, my own secretary buzzed me to say that Gentry was on the other line.

His voice sounded like a graveyard of chains. When he asked if I could meet him in an hour, I presumed that he meant at the Club, but without explanation, he proposed a rendezvous at Saint Joseph's Oratory on the mountain. Looking north through my office window, thirty floors above the street, I surveyed Mount Royal in the pouring rain, and prepared for heavy weather.

# 19

AMID UNDULATING SCALES OF dark umbrellas shielding indomitable tourists, I climbed toward the summit of the windswept mountain in search of my enigmatic mark. The Oratory dome appeared in the mist like a capsized dirigible, whose titanic proportions were second only to Saint Peter's Basilica in Rome. Seas of passing faces, hermetically sealed in waxen hats and raingear, finally gave way to a stoic, chiseled face, looking out into the rain.

With his hands plunged into an olive duster, he watched east from the shining walk, as though he were searching for something he had lost that he feared he might not find again. His flaxen hair scattered in the gusting rain, and his spectacles were fogged by the rain. At no more than fifty meters from my destination, he stood there like a captain at the bowsprit—awaiting my ascent as a sorry second mate who had been freshly rescued from the brine.

"Look what the cat dragged in," Gentry stoically acknowledged my arrival. Scrutinizing my pathetic state, it was as though he wasn't sure who it was. In the eerie silence, save a flock of geese mournfully calling overhead, he cast his eyes downtown toward the stalagmitic towers, rising in the falling rain.

"It's over!" Gentry called, through the teeming rain.

"What's over?" I rhetorically called back.

He winced—as if to say that I knew better than to ask.

"It's a building and a subway stop!" I said.

"It used to be the church," he dismissed the appeal—as though I had missed the point.

"I would feel betrayed," I had to confess.

"It's not about you or I," he said.

As the rain rapped hollow on his canvas duster, I wondered why he was surprised. Having seen this film a hundred times before in my own narcissistic profession, I had always assumed it was par for the course in a world whose given instinct was to win. Puzzled as I was by why anyone would bet his life on an institution, Gentry telepathically looked me in the eye and replied: "I thought the church was different."

Unlike Gentry, and the Greatest Generation on both sides of the Atlantic, I was born too late to invest my faith in any institution. Offended as I was by the underhanded tactics Beringer had clearly employed, I nonetheless had to sympathize with the predicament the Dean was in. Gentry seemed to me unnecessarily troubled by what I thought of as a rational response to an economic challenge objectively imposed by this increasingly secular time.

A sudden squall of rain swept around the mountain in a horizontal report. The gargantuan Oratory dome ominously loomed in the mist, reducing our presence on the desolate landscape to notable insignificance. Our strained exchanges were swallowed by the wind as we heeled into the driving rain—when I realized something else was bothering him that he needed to explain.

"When I was a young priest!" Gentry called again, into the wind and the rain. "A man appeared to me out of the mist—up here, on a day like this!"

"I was wearing a collar," he robotically went on, "and he asked if I would hear his confession."

Nodding at a low stone wall, he said, "We sat down over there. I heard the usual things—lies, transgressions, the inevitable regrets—before he turned white as a sheet, as though he knew he was going to die."

As incredible as the story seemed, blood was coursing through my veins. However skeptical I should have been, I knew that he was telling the truth. When I asked what happened then, I already knew he couldn't tell the rest of the story—as if it had given rise to some grief that was too much for him to bear.

A gust of wind enfolded the collar of the duster around the back of his neck. "The only thing he said was, he was out in the cold—and that he couldn't be brought back in! When I asked him if someone was trying . . ." and the rest was lost in a crescendo of rain.

I wondered if Gentry had forgotten I was there as he stared down the side of the mountain—or just couldn't fathom how such a thing could happen, even in the driving rain. Plunging his hands into his hollow duster, he cast a sidelong glance into the trees. So I felt compelled to pronounce the final verdict: "And you never saw him again."

"He turned there on the walk . . ." his voice tremored, and cracked. "And he . . . called to me—through the rain. 'Thank you,' he said, 'for being my brother!' And I never saw him again."

For the first time since Gentry had retreated to that past, he turned and looked directly at me. "And thank you," he said, just short of a petition. "Thank you for being my brother."

I told him it was nothing. He told me that when you're out in the cold, it can mean everything. Watching him descending the walk toward the trees, terror telegraphed through my frame, and before he disappeared, I pathetically offered my help through the teeming rain.

"Beringer is going to want to talk!" he called.

"He knows that you and I are friends!" I said.

"Is that what we are?"

I swallowed hard. "That's what we are!" I said.

I decided to go back to my pedestrian office in search of some normalcy. After an hour of looking through the window at the mountain through the pouring rain, I concluded that the Dean was simply doing his job in an impossible situation. Sympathetic as I was to Gentry as a friend, I believed that he was unrealistic—because as laudable as his ideals may have been, I knew that they could be his end.

Leaving the office, I felt reassured by this reasonable conclusion. Although I wanted to avoid a confrontation with the Dean of Christ Church Cathedral, I looked forward to what I anticipated would be a reassuring explanation. In fact, when I got home it was Beringer's voice soothing my answering machine—asking me to call his secretary in hopes of getting together.

# 20

THE DEAN'S ASSISTANT WAS expecting my call when I phoned his office in the morning. She asked if I was free that afternoon, and we made the appointment for four. Leaving early from work, I was warmly welcomed and offered "a spot of tea," before being shown to a chair outside his door, where I heard him on the telephone.

Uncertain that he saw me, I felt uneasy in the eavesdropper's catbird seat. Struggling to hear as little as I could, I therefore heard most everything. As he wound up the call, I deduced that he was speaking with a friend, or counsel of advice—to whom he attributed "Godly wisdom in these unfortunately worldly matters."

Having thanked him so profusely that I could have inferred he was speaking with Jesus himself, Beringer ended with a curious crack: "Yes . . . one stone and two birds." In an instant he was standing at the open door, where I got up to an earnest handshake, and a full-blown, "Benjamin!" which vacuumed me into the large Victorian office. Behind a generous desk leaned a pair of sculling oars obediently stationed in the corner, before row upon row of dusty leather books that culminated in the Harvard Classics.

"An old friend from Yale Divinity," he said, "who was just elected Bishop!" With an ambiguous nod, he went on to enthuse: "Rory's quite a character!" Confused by the seeming change in attitude toward his erstwhile confidante, I might have interpreted Beringer's smile as a less than unqualified endorsement.

"Let me read you his profile!" Beringer said, leaning back against his desk. Donning a pair of tortoiseshell glasses, which looked conspicuously like Gentry's, Beringer bore down on Rory's narrative like an admiring younger brother. The best I can recollect is the following: "I was like every other Princeton undergraduate—intelligent, athletic, and agnostic—whose

God was success, and the pleasures it brought when I arrived on Wall Street. So, when I won the Rhodes and went to Oxford, life was all about me."

Inviting me to sit, he continued to presume my interest in Rory's resumé. "During that year," Beringer read on, "I sensed that there was something more. Yet my need for adventure was not about God—but for the dying things of this world. I chased a succession of empty careers: a cowboy on a ranch in Venezuela; a barfly in Bogota; a groom at the Polo Club in Newport, Rhode Island; and finally, a New York actor."

"What's a barfly?"

"He's honest if he's anything!" Beringer ignored my question.

"What sort of actor?"

"I'm not sure," he replied. "I believe it was dinner theater."

Picturing Rory as an overzealous convert, I asked, "Were you close at Yale?"

Looking nearly offended, Beringer laughed. "Rory is an evangelical!" Arching his eyebrows, he almost smirked. "Now, they're a different breed of cat!"

I had to agree with him about that. "How would you describe yourself?"

"A broad-church liberal!" he roundly pronounced.

"A little bit of everything?" I asked.

"You might say that!" he endorsed my conclusion. "So long as Christ is at the center!"

As one who had never perceived the ministry as a bona fide "profession," my curiosity got the better of me: "What led you to become a priest?"

"Who!" I stood corrected.

"Who?" I inquired.

"God called me, kicking and screaming!"

"How did you know—"

"That it wasn't a wrong number? When I realized it was all that I could do!"

"I would think you could have done a thousand things," I said.

He enjoyed the vote of confidence. "Not when the offer comes from up there!"

Together we peered at the ceiling.

"Ben, I need to confide in you," he said, his eyes returning to my chair. "As much as I have prayed that it could have been different, the Cathedral is in dire financial straits. I don't mean to imply anyone deceived me before

I accepted the job. I have prayed we could survive without the building project, but without it—we're not sustainable."

Almost imperceptibly, his eyes suggested tears, if not inconsolable regret. As much as I resented how it had been handled, in the interest of protecting Gentry's interest I wanted to explore Beringer's designs in the hope of a compromise. I'd even managed to envision "Bishop Stephen Gentry" etched in stone somewhere in the complex—however well I knew that Gentry was the last man on the planet ever to be bribed.

"I think I understand," I reflectively began—to launch the negotiation.

Like a marionette whose string had been pulled, Beringer jolted off his desk, and striding over with an outstretched hand, rejoiced: "I knew you would!"

It was as though I'd just agreed to lay the cornerstone.

"And blessings!" he pronounced with finality, pumping me up from my chair. To this day I wonder if it was too many years at the Cabot dinner table, or the starched intimidation of a clerical collar bearing down on my tie, but as easy as it would have been to call the Dean on this underhanded tactic, I allowed myself to be carried to the door in the spirit of propriety. Yet in retrospect these were just self-serving excuses for pursuing the path of least resistance—if not a sign, my reputation notwithstanding, of an outright lack of courage.

Nearing the door, my eyes were tempted by a photograph on the wall. Amidst a tapestry of honors, gilded diplomas, and ordination certificates, I was taken by a handsome sepia print that looked like it was shot in the forties. A solitary sculler in a wooden racing shell on a magnificently tranquil river was resting his arms on a pair of slender oars, with his head barely bowed, as if in prayer.

"Is that your father?"

Beringer laughed. "Do I look that old?

"No need!" he presumed an apology. "I'm told I'm a chip off the old block!"

"Is your father a priest?"

"My father was a salesman! And yours?"

"My father is a lawyer."

"Sometimes the apple doesn't fall far from the tree!"

"No," I said. "Sometimes it doesn't."

# 21

I called Gentry's office at nine the next morning to the snarl of the Bishop's bulldog. Though nothing new, she seemed newly determined to keep outsiders out. The name "Ben Cabot" had little effect as she explained he was out of town—"on Bishop's retreat"—spawning in my mind angling on the Miramichi River.

The truth is, I feared that I had sold Gentry out. An objective observer might have perceived my passive acquiescence as a tactical detachment not unbecoming of an able advocate and lawyer. If my father was right that men had two ears and one mouth, and so should listen twice as much as they should speak, in this case my unconscionable silence was a sign that I had lacked the will.

On Sunday morning I went to church in hopes of finding Gentry. As he was nowhere to be seen, I avoided the Dean and slipped out through the chancel door. After packing for a week-long trip out of town, I put in a call to Boston, and hearing my father's reassuring voice, unleashed my diatribe.

"Not to add fuel to the fire," my father said, "but I did hear something mildly disconcerting."

"What?" I demanded.

"Relax, Ben," he replied. "He's a liberal—just not in Copley Square."

Ben Sr. was a master at reminding his friends of their shared hypocrisies. Making a sport of infuriating likeminded liberals, he coined the phrase, and Cabot self-critique: "Think left, live right." What always set him apart in my mind from his similarly prosperous siblings was his need to question his own integrity twice as much as their own.

"The word is, Trinity had a problem with the homeless sleeping in the pews. With the blessing of the Vestry, he developed a plan to charge admission at the door."

"Jesus Christ . . ."

"I doubt it," he said. "Christ couldn't have afforded the ticket."

When my silence went too long, my father went on, "Ben, it's always in the water. The only thing worse than a deceptive liberal is an honest conservative."

In that moment I wished I had been bequeathed his capacity for self-critique. "Do you remember," I asked, "how the headmaster at Latin said I had an authority problem?"

I guessed he was smiling.

"Do you think . . . I do?"

Then came my father's classic pause. "There is some authority," Ben Sr. mused, "with which you ought to have a problem."

"What about the church?"

The pause prolonged to silence. "That's for you to answer," he said.

Night was falling when I hung up the phone. However confident I may have been in the game of high-stakes litigation, I felt lucky that I would never have to face Beringer in the courtroom. Then, realizing it was Sunday evening, I jumped up from my chair, and broke out into the late September air in search of levelheaded counsel.

When I arrived on Place d'Armes, the last of Cathedral in the Night had gone into the van. A preoccupied Hale was closing the doors, as a figure I guessed to be Henri was talking at the priest while dangling a cardboard box from the handle in his hand. As I approached, the box came into view as a beautifully rendered little church; even at a distance it was obvious that its creator was a talented artist.

"You look like you've seen a ghost!" Hale called.

I laughed. "Is that what it was?"

Henri looked genuinely glad to see me, and came over to shake my hand. When I pointed to the box, he held it in the air for me to behold his creation: an arched paper door, delicately bolted with a miniscule metal lock; paper doily windows, intricately mimicking Gothic tracery; and a red tin roof, lavishly scrawled with what looked like a biblical verse. I scrutinized the scrawl: "Jesus était sans abri"—in English, "Jesus was homeless."

As though he had decided the tour was over, Henri put the church on the ground. Standing up again, he drew out a folder from his oily, threadbare jacket. He flopped it open and discreetly displayed a sheaf of pencil drawings—exquisitely depicting all sorts and conditions of people on the streets of Montreal.

Unsettled as I was by the melancholic faces and slope-shouldered profiles of the poor, what was more disturbing was the unexpected sorrow of the prosperous pedestrians. Moved as I was by the truth of what he'd drawn with pencil lead on tattered paper, I knew that anyone who saw what Henri saw, was able to see through me. But before I could respond, he closed the grimy folder and slipped it back into his jacket—and with an enigmatic smile and nod of his head, he picked up his church and was gone.

"You look like you need a drink!" Hale said. "I'm a full-blooded bachelor tonight!"

I tried not to jump to the self-serving conclusion.

"Claire is with her family in Westmount!"

Getting over the romantic disappointment, I was on my way with Hale to the Plateau. Duluth was lined with red brick houses, reminiscent of its working-class past—backing onto alleyways scattered with drunks and random student bicycles. The diminutive scale of the neighborhood evoked a movie set: sporadically illuminated here and there by streetlamps spilling light onto the walks.

We approached what looked like an abandoned church on the corner of Saint Denis. At first I thought he was dropping something off before bringing me to his apartment. But something in the habitual way he leapt up the worn stone steps made me realize that this house of worship was also Hale's residence.

"No shit," I said. "You live in a church?"

"Not as a going concern."

"This is—home?" I asked, as he unlocked the door.

"It's a place to lay my head," he said.

Hale led me up the wooden stairs to the second-floor parish hall, and throwing an industrial double-pole switch, welcomed me into the space. I followed him across the expansive wooden floor toward a steel cot and table in the corner. Before I arrived, I noted a platoon of sleeping bags, coats, hats, and socks.

"You run a shelter too?"

"Don't tell the Bishop. Only in the dead of winter."

"Why would he care?"

"He doesn't," Hale replied. "But the Trustees seem to care a lot."

"So, you live in a church," I stupidly repeated.

"Where do you live?" he asked.

"Westmount," I imparted.

"That's a nice part of town."

"I grew up in a nice part of town."

"So did I," he said. "It's hard to leave home."

"I always hated leaving home," I said.

"Was it hard for you?" I finally asked.

"I'm not sure I ever had one."

# 22

HALE DRAGGED OUT THE single chair from the desk, and offered me a seat. As he dropped to the cot, he took a sterling flask from under a sorry-looking pillow. The olive drab mountain of winterwear and military camping equipment made the otherwise ecclesiastical space look more like a commissary.

On the strength of my first sip of Canadian Club, I asked, "Who's your decorator?"

"Salvation Army!" Hale easily imparted, taking back the flask. "Except for the microwave."

"Nice piece," I agreed—to which he took a healthy swig.

"Dumpster," he confessed, handing me the flagon.

I burned another nip. "Had it for long?"

"Long enough to know how to use it," he blustered.

"What do you use it for?"

"Indigestion, mostly."

"I suspect we went to the same—cooking school," I snorted. "Who the hell cooks for Cathedral in the Night?"

"I do," he said. "In the basement."

"Every Sunday?"

"Every Sunday. My excuse for not going to church."

As weary as Hale looked, I couldn't help but wonder how he did what he did: what it was in his past, or what he hoped for in the future, that inspired him to go on. Yet despite its evident liabilities, somehow I envied his life. Having grown up assuming I had won the capricious lottery of birth—the one that presumes life's crowning achievement is holding on to what he's got—I realized what had been taken from me was the gift of an uncertain future, whose ambiguous freedom beckons its prey to discover that they can fly.

"Why did you go to Vietnam?" I asked.

He handed back the flask.

"I heard the Mekong Delta was as scary as it got."

"It wasn't a water park," he said.

"Do you think," I asked him, feeling the buzz, "God ever gives you more than you can handle?"

"What do you mean, more?"

"Too much," I replied.

"It's always too much," he said.

"So, why do you do it?"

"If it weren't too much, I wouldn't do it," he said.

"What was the hardest—'too much'?" I asked.

Hale winced. "For as many limbs as I had to bury, I never got over the kids."

I recalled the celebrated photograph of the skinny, naked little girl, running down the road, screaming with the pain of napalm burning on her back. As poignant as it was to see the agony disfiguring her beautiful face, what I would never forget was her utter innocence that one feared would never come again. More unbearable still than the futility of running to escape the pain, was trying to explain to an innocent child why anyone would do such a thing.

"You didn't come home," I finally said.

"I did—for a time," he said.

"You didn't stay," I said.

"It wasn't home," he said.

"So, you went to the Amazon."

"I was looking for something to believe in," he said.

"I don't know how you can believe in anything."

He looked at me. "I don't know how you can't," he said.

"What do you believe in?" I asked.

"I believe in life."

"That covers a lot of territory."

"Less than you think." Hale took back the flask, and burned another nip. "There are two Greek words in the Gospels for 'life'—*psuche* and *zoe*," he said. "*Psuche* refers to the life of the body—the breath and pulse that keeps the party going. *Zoe* refers to vitality. To animation—to the spirit. Whenever Jesus talked about 'eternal life', the word he always used was *zoe*."

"No shit," I said.

"No shit," he said.

84

"So, where do you find this *zoe*?"

Hale thought for a moment. "On the margins."

"That sounds like a long way from the church."

"Probably because it is," he replied.

"So—what's the purpose of the church?"

Hale slyly grinned. "Maybe to remind us that we always have to leave."

I was already laughing. If it was clear that Hale was half in the bag, I was all the way in. Taking back the flask, its negligible weight suggested we were near the end.

"What was it like—being a shaman?"

"Apprentice to a shaman," Hale said.

"I knew a guy who went to the Amazon," I crowed, "for an Ayahuasca ritual."

"It can be used for recreation," he granted.

"He said it was powerful stuff."

Hale nodded.

"Like having a sixth sense," I said.

Hale faintly shook his head. "For me . . . it just sharpened the senses I had. You see . . . connections," he reflected.

"Connections . . ." I repeated.

"Patterns . . . and connections. Between animals and plants. Rocks . . . and people.

"My mentor has been talking with the river spirits for eighty years," he mused. "There is this giant freshwater whale he brings up . . . so the fish will come in behind it."

"Do they . . . really come?" I blearily queried.

"They seem to . . . yeah," Hale said.

Even tanked, he sensed my skepticism.

"If the things Cessario said didn't happen, it wouldn't be believable. When Cessario talks, people listen. He's gained his credibility over the years from being accurate."

"But is it . . . a real whale?" I insisted.

"It depends on who you talk to," Hale said. "Every tribe in the Amazon has this whale . . . but no biologist has found it. You hear about these whales from all the shamans . . . and you see them everywhere in paintings. But you can't set a trap, or drop a giant hook and catch it. So, you ask—are they real?"

"I'm asking," I said.

He groggily looked up: "They sure as hell are real to them!"

It was apparent to us both that we were stinking drunk.

"Do you remember the story of Jesus . . ." Hale said, "calling up the fish to Peter's boat?"

"I remember—fishing nets."

"You're a goddam scholar. Kind of like that," he said.

"I've always been partial to pigeons," I said.

"Pigeons!" Hale came back.

"These rich kids I knew . . . used to kick the pigeons' asses . . . out on the Esplanade," I said.

"The Esplanade," Hale said.

"Yeah, the Esplanade."

"Rich, you say?"

"Yeah, pretty rich."

Hale vaguely nodded.

"It kind of . . . broke my heart," I slurred. "Especially the weak ones."

Hale was silent.

"Somehow it always seemed . . . it was the weak ones who mattered most."

"Because . . ." Hale said, "without the weak ones . . . the rest of us are lost."

"I always thought you swore too much to be a priest," I said.

"Really!" he responded.

"Priests," I explained, "are not supposed to swear."

"What about Jesus?" he retorted.

Even in my stupor, I could tell that Hale had something up his biblical sleeve.

"When the Pharisees got pissed at the disciples," he said, "for not washing their hands before they ate, he told them not to worry about what was unclean that went down into the sewer."

I was waiting for the other shoe to drop, when he concluded, "Only . . . he didn't say 'sewer.'"

"What did he say?"

"'Shithole,'" Hale replied.

"What—did he say?" I asked.

"'Shithole'. The Aramaic word for 'sewer' is closer to the English word 'shithole.'"

"Do you eat with that same mouth?"

Hale smiled. "We all do! That's the point of Communion."

"I've never understood the point of Communion."

"There is no point. It's . . . a practice."

"Then I've never understood the practice of Communion."

"It's a practice—that changes the heart."

"So, it's not about the host . . . that goes into the mouth, and down into the sewer," I said.

"It's only bread," Hale said, "until it changes the heart."

"It's a miracle you lasted this long."

"Or a miracle the church has lasted this long."

"How long do you think it will last?"

"What does it matter?"

"What does it matter? If it doesn't last, it's gone!"

"Permanence has nothing to do with it," he said. "Jesus wasn't permanent."

"So, how did he last?"

"There's a difference between being permanent . . . and eternal."

"What about our Dean?" I free-associated.

"Like the rest of them," Hale said.

"Like the rest of them?"

"Like the rest of them. Born to wear the purple diapers."

"That doesn't bother you?"

"A peafowl is a peafowl. They're always running for something. Are you going to his art show?"

"His art show," I inquired.

"You haven't been to church!" Hale said.

"When is it?"

"Friday night at the Cathedral."

"Are you going?" I asked.

"I'm bringing Henri."

I deliberated.

"Claire will be there," he said.

I balked—then gave in to his mischievous grin. "That isn't fair," I said.

Unsteadily standing, I sashayed a retreat across the slanting floor, looking forward to the crisp autumn air, and long aerobic walk back to Westmount. As I made my way down the treacherous stairs, I was glad Hale was safely behind me. Landing on the walk, I turned to see him watching with unabashed amusement.

"Hale!" I called.

"Ben!" he called back.

"I always thought heaven—" and faltered.

"Thought heaven—what?"

"I always thought heaven was—three hundred miles up in the air!"

"And don't tell me!" he said. "You also thought heaven is where you go when you die!"

I stumbled on the walk. "When—the hell else?"

"For Christ's sake, Ben! Heaven's now!"

Making my way toward Saint Denis, I managed to turn around again. "Hale!" I yelled.

"Ben!" he yelled back.

"What the hell's a peafowl?"

His laughter awoke the wee small hours of the morning. "A peacock!" he finally cried.

Cackling like an asthmatic hyena, I almost tripped again. When I reached the last lamp in the neighborhood, I turned in its pool of light. As I watched him keeping vigil on the granite steps like a sentry in the night, thinking of all the people I knew that I had once thought of as my friends, for the first time in my life I realized what it meant to have someone who truly had my back—and that when all was said and done, and our successes had failed, all that would be left would be our friends.

"Hale!" I called.

"Ben!" he called back.

"Do you have a brother?"

"Of course I have a brother!"

"What's his name?"

"His name is Ben!" Hale cried.

"No!" I waved him off. "I mean—a real brother!"

"You look pretty real to me!"

The truth is, I choked.

"So, do I have a brother?"

"Yes," I cried. "A—real brother!"

# 23

PER HALE'S INSTRUCTIONS, I was stationed at the door of Cathedral House at five o'clock. Several minutes later my compatriots appeared, with Henri leading the way. Pumping my arm like a coupling rod on an antique steam locomotive, he looked almost surprised to catch the likes of me on this toney side of town.

The sartorial flow of Episcopalians passing the three of us made me wish I had been able to go home and change out of my three-piece suit. Standing in the doorway was Beringer, with the familiar Senior Warden: a tall drink of water accompanied by a woman who had to be his wife. Instantly, Beringer came forward to greet me as though we were life-long friends—practically giving me a slap on the back before making the introduction.

"Wes, I'd like you to meet Ben Cabot—a fellow expatriate!"

"Well, we won't hold that against you!" Wes jested, enjoying his amusing remark.

"Ben is practicing the law," the Dean remarked.

"The name of the firm?" Wes inquired. Wes seemed impressed. "Wes Westmoreland! And I'd like to introduce my wife, Tinka!"

He was a deprecating Brit, with distinctly carded hair resolutely pasted to his scalp. I noted a tapered meerschaum pipe cupped in his left hand, along with a tawny suggestion of tobacco tinging the corner of his mouth. Imagining his elegant "Canadian" pipe clenched in his equine teeth, I guessed if it had gone into an errant orifice it probably would have snapped.

I was about to ask Wes what he "did" when I realized I didn't care. Whatever it was seemed irrelevant. Whatever endowment may have sustained his elegant, understated life, certainly derived from the selfsame system that unjustly sustained my own.

When I noticed Wes tortuously craning his neck, I guessed that he was watching Henri. Putting a hand on Henri's shoulder, Hale steered him clear of his detractor, and with Claire, withdrew to the gallery walls to survey Beringer's work. Wes furtively turned to the artist and host with a furrow of genuine concern—selflessly confessing, with bated breath: "I should probably take care of this."

"Henri is my guest," I interrupted our familiar old-boy huddle.

"Well, of course he is!" Wes retorted. "I just wanted to be sure! We have problems, you know," he confided in me. "Even at the Cathedral!"

He could see his obsequious apology went over like a fart in church. The tribal pact dissolved. Picking up the pace, Wes smoothly moved on to the virtues of his fabulous wife, raving, "Tinka put together the entire exhibit in just a matter of three weeks!"

"With Rob's help!" Tinka swooned. "Thanks to Rob, it wasn't difficult!"

Tinka's womanly form and silver hair—verging on a hue of blue—gave me to guess Wes was one of those men who had successfully married his mother. As Beringer and his Senior Warden withdrew for further conversation, Tinka had me cornered in the misplaced hope of advancing her social interests. Describing her trials of maintaining four houses, she divulged the brilliant tactic of renovating four identical kitchens so she would know where the spices went.

It was one of those confusing non sequiturs which for a moment almost make sense—until one sits down with pen and paper and tries to deconstruct the logic. I suspected that imparting the strategy was less to communicate her brilliance than to recapitulate her argument to Wes for renovating four kitchens. In any case, she managed to convey the two Westmorelands had four houses before finally divining my disinterest in kitchens and bidding me a pleasant exhibit.

But thanks to Tinka's philanthropic effort—"A Trinity of Sacred Spaces"—the commodious hall brimmed with leaders from the diocese and the city. The exhibit was composed of an impressive array of oil and pastel works, elegantly hung in gilded frames along the expansive walls. Setting out in search of my lost contingent somewhere in the swelling throng, I seized the chance to assess Beringer's artistic talent on my own.

My immediate response was that these were paintings people of means would want to buy. If they wouldn't be mistaken for works of art in any unaffected sense, they would have been at home in a corporate boardroom, or above my fireplace. Most impressive of all was Beringer's chameleonic aptitude to render impressionism, romanticism, and realism, all in one.

Nevertheless, I was technically impressed, and was preparing to let him know when I looked across the room to see Henri kneeling before the Dean. Relieved to discover he was only in the process of unpacking his cardboard church, I watched as Beringer gawked from on high, in a bowtie reminiscent of the fifties. Thanks to Henri's paucity of English, the Dean looked oblivious—though nodding with such sincerity one would have sworn Henri had a convert.

Claire intervened with angelic grace. As Henri unhooked the red cardboard door, Claire expressed his conviction that in light of the fact that Jesus was homeless, churches should never be locked. Watching his intrigue rise and fall with Claire's melodic voice, I felt both sympathetic with the Dean's fascination, and annoyed by his arrogance.

"I'm Rob!" he pronounced, overarching Henri to meet Claire's unassuming hand. Short of, "Aw, shucks," he had taken on the charmingly boyish demeanor of one who was surprised, if not astonished, by how he ended up in this position. In her Claire McWilliams way, Claire consented to a handshake before leaning back against Hale—as if to convey that as pleasant as he seemed, she had very different plans.

In the interest of righting a listing ship, I expressed my appreciation for Beringer's monumental effort in producing the ambitious one-man show. Taking my remark as a compliment, he slightly overplayed his hand, explaining that the work was "thankfully sustained by a fortuitous grant I won." He thoughtfully recounted how the Tuscany pastels were done while on sabbatical, whereas the Boston cityscapes had been rendered when Rector of Trinity Church, Copley Square.

If Picasso was right—that art is a lie that makes us realize the truth—Beringer's work portrayed a truth that somehow realized a lie. It was not that he lacked the ability to render convincing images. It was rather that, however accurately rendered, somehow they were not true.

I wondered if Beringer's disregard of Hale was due to having already met, or whether it was simply a consequence of Hale's inconsequence. In either case, Hale didn't seem to care as he watched Beringer's flirtation—visibly amused by what he must have known was a futile romantic effort. Averting his eyes from Claire's rebuff, he finally acknowledged Hale, as though he felt relieved from the arduous duty of being the center of attention.

"It's a noble work you do!" Beringer pronounced. "And a work that is close to my heart!"

"Glad to hear it," Hale replied. "We need all the friends we can get."

"Count me as a friend!" Beringer applauded, discreetly glancing at Claire. "Personally, I'd like to see Cathedral in the Nights all across the city!"

Like the telltale crank of a starting car, he intoned the end of his visit. With sincerest regret, Beringer explained "the unfortunate need to circulate." Vociferously thanking the three of us for coming, he literally overlooked Henri, who was kneeling on the floor and preoccupied with packing up the carboard church.

"I'll have to get down to Cathedral in the Night!" he said, shaking Hale's hand. "Ben!" he turned to me. "And nice to meet you Claire! You do have a blessed smile."

Watching Beringer crossing the room, I realized that I hadn't seen Gentry. It was less that I expected the Bishop to be present than that I wondered why he was absent. In spite of his incontestable position as the sovereign of the diocese, I was oddly reminded of the grade school chum who mysteriously disappears in summer.

Taking a step back, I opened my eyes to a room full of elated priests. Unable to discern what was afoot as the Dean was being courted like a Bishop, I could see how clergy and laity alike were charmed by their engaging host. If he served at their behest, it was by the selfsame secret of any monarch's success: the subjects whom he served were as invested in the king as the king was invested in himself.

# 24

As we were leaving, I told Hale I would like to take our foursome out to dinner. Informing me that Claire had an overnight shift and had to go home to sleep, he explained that Henri had lost his apartment, and had a shelter curfew to meet. After kissing Claire goodbye, he suggested that we walk Henri to the Brewery Mission, and together the three of us descended Saint Laurent to the bowels of Old Montreal.

The truth is, I felt almost offended by the way Hale conveyed this news. The fact that Henri was homeless again should have been the first thing on his mind; yet he didn't appear to be especially surprised, and Henri seemed already past it. As I listened to Henri agonize over not having thanked the Dean—distracted as he was, he belabored the point, by packing up his cardboard church—I couldn't help but wonder why some men pass through life with an embarrassment of riches, while others, by circumstance, chance, or accident, pass through battered sheltered doors.

As we were walking, I asked Henri what he had thought of Beringer's paintings.

"Très joli," he said. "Très, très, très joli!": "Very pretty—very, very pretty!"

"But do you think they're good?" I curiously asked.

Self-consciously, Henri looked at Hale.

"Les tableaux," Hale said, encouraging him.

He sheepishly smiled. "Non," he said.

"Non?" I incredulously laughed.

"You asked him!" Hale retorted.

I wasn't prepared for an honest answer. "So, the answer is, 'No'?"

Henri looked embarrassed, before looking up. "Oui, la réponse est, non."

"Why not?" I pursued him.

Henri peered at Hale.

"Dis lui!" Hale insisted.

I managed to follow most of what he said, save the repeated word, *ame*. When I asked Hale what *ame* meant, he deferred to Henri—who finally nodded his consent. Looking back to me, Hale imparted, "Henri thinks the paintings lack a soul."

For all my own superficial assessments of Beringer's pretty paintings—from the kind of room where they would best be hung, to the bourgeois clients who would buy them—what I had missed was what Henri understood as the reason they were no good: that however fetching the paintings may have been, somehow they lacked a soul.

"You're an artist," I told him.

Henri looked embarrassed.

"I mean it," I insisted.

I was going to ask if I could buy one of his drawings, but thankfully something stopped me. Something told me they were not for sale. Almost as painful as Henri's poverty staring me in the face, was my futile attempt to reach into my pocket to buy my way out of my own.

Leaving Henri at the battered door to spend a night in that mayhem, I was overwhelmed by a poignant sadness that had nothing to do with pity. If I didn't know whence the sadness had come, it was long before Henri. What I only knew was there was something I had missed by the hapless ambitions of my life, which defied everything I'd ever been taught about success as the way to fulfillment.

In spite of the perennial crowds of tourists that frequented Saint-Gabriel, the oldest inn in North America was worth the spectacle. The honeyed air of autumn ushered us in beneath the turning trees, and thanks to our early arrival we finagled a table in front of a fire. Glad to hear that dinner was on me, Hale joined me in a Maker's Mark, and together we took in heady fumes of bourbon in the grotto of stone and timber.

"I'm sorry Henri couldn't make it," I said.

"So is Henri," Hale said.

"It's hard to see him on the street again."

"It's harder on him," he said.

"It's getting cold," I said.

"At least he's in a shelter."

"I couldn't do it," I said.

"Have you ever lived outside?" I asked.

"Only by choice," he said. He paused. "But that's not living outside."

"What is it?"

"That's vacation."

Feeling under siege, I had all I could do to hold my precarious position.

"I have a guy who hasn't lain down in six years because he's afraid of getting jumped. The only 'inside' he knows is the hospital, where he gets treated for his swollen feet. At least he hasn't lost them. But one day he will—one day he'll lose them both."

"So, what the hell are we supposed to do!" I exploded.

"Be there," Hale calmly replied.

"And what does that achieve!"

"Who said anything about achievement?"

"Me!" I retaliated, gulping down my bourbon.

He looked me directly in the eye.

"Achievement . . . is so deep in my bones," I confessed, "I don't think I could live without it."

Hale mischievously smiled. "I remember breaking up a fight one night between two of the guys. One punched the other one in the mouth, and had him bleeding like a faucet. And I remember thinking—until now I almost had as many teeth as I had parishioners."

Unsuccessfully suppressing a belly laugh, I realized the joke was on me. Every one of my clients had a mouth full of teeth that were as handsome as their phony smiles. And for all my equally handsome ambitions, I knew that so did I.

"The other night you said something that didn't add up."

"I told you—you're no good at addition."

"That despite everything you saw in Vietnam, you had no choice but to believe."

"Not in spite of, but because of," Hale said.

"I'm still no good at addition."

"You said you've seen the photograph, 'Napalm Girl'. She was saved by the photographer. Flame boats shooting fire two fucking hundred yards up and down the Mekong River have been replaced by the largest floating market of fruit and vegetables in the world. And go to Hoi An, where some of the worst fighting of the War took place. The streets are filled with lanterns, people celebrating, and having families again.

"And craziest of all, is the absence of hard feelings. When I went back—it was over. So you ask, how can you believe in life? I don't know how the hell you can't."

As I watched Hale attacking his Porterhouse steak like a wild boar in the jungle, I wondered how he managed to endure what had become a feminized institution. If churchgoers were leaving the pews in droves, most of them were men, and those that remained came on the tether of their overbearing wives. Yet there was something about him that wouldn't have survived any institution—whose inevitable rules served to suppress every natural instinct but fear.

While we were growing up, earning college credits and banking on successful careers, Hale must have been lost to his dangerous dreams that were doomed everywhere but in his mind. I grieved to think how long this one would last before the inescapable darkness would one day overcome the impossible light that illumined Cathedral in the Night. For the first time, the fact that Jesus's ministry lasted for no more than three years was unutterably real—and an unutterable loss that was waiting to happen again.

"Why do you do it?" I finally asked.

"It's the only game that pays," he said.

"So, you do it for yourself."

"I do it for myself."

"Which means, you're selfish," I said.

He peered at me with his enigmatic smile, and he said: "Selfish as hell."

"So, Jesus was selfish as hell," I said.

"Selfish as hell," he said.

"You could have had more teeth than parishioners," I said.

"I could have been successful," Hale said.

"I can't remember when I didn't want to be successful."

"It's a harvest of dust," he said. "Ever hear of the monk, Thomas Merton?"

"He wrote *The Seven Storey Mountain*."

"After the book made him famous, Merton said, 'Be anything you like, be madmen, drunks, and bastards of every shape and form, but at all costs avoid one thing—success.'"

"So much for our generation," I said, hoping to deflect my own indictment.

Hale wasn't going to let me off the hook. "'If you're too obsessed with success,' Merton said, 'you will forget to live. If you learned only how to be a success, your life has probably been wasted.'"

Needless to say, this wasn't the affirmation I was looking for. "How the hell have you survived the church?" I said.

"I didn't know I had," he replied.

"Then how have you managed to believe in God?" I said.

"Is that what I believe in?" he asked.

"So, what do you believe in?"

"I believe in Jesus."

"What the hell's the difference?"

Hale shrugged his shoulders. "There is no difference."

"You *are* a goddam heretic," I said.

"What's a heretic? From the Greek, a heretic is someone who is 'free to choose.'"

"You're lucky to have Gentry as your Bishop," I said.

"For as long as we have him," Hale said.

"That sounds ominous."

"You were there tonight."

"Gentry wasn't."

"Exactly.

"Isn't Beringer a friend of yours?" he asked.

"Beringer is no friend," I said.

"I'm not surprised," Hale said.

"Why is that?" I asked.

"Beringer doesn't want a friend."

# 25

SOMETHING HAPPENS IN MONTREAL with the melancholic turning of autumn that doesn't seem to happen in places that won't know the unrelenting grip of winter. Preparing for the worst, the city has no choice but to celebrate the golden moments of fragrant, sweet decay, which beckons men like me to entertain mortality. Café tables gleaming beneath a failing sun in defiance of the coming solstice fill the autumn evenings with beautiful women, provoking captivated partners.

In those dumbfounded days, when I retreated from the helter-skelter of religious ambitions, the only sanctuary that commanded my respect was the one I feared I had betrayed. If in Beringer's world, the likes of Cathedral in the Night had no value, my own complicity and convenient neglect may have put a community in peril. Bewildered by how far the church had come from the wandering ministry of Jesus, I wondered how far it had to go to dream the dreams that were dreamed two thousand years ago.

An unexpected warmth at the beginning of November was a waft of southern grace—if not an unexpected gift outright I should have been leery to receive. It was raining when I passed the misted café windows in the elegant uptown hotels, and descended toward the knells of distant river barges and the sonorous tolling of bells. Fog crept on the cobbles in the streets and alleyways that meandered up from the river, anticipating the day beyond the fall, which promises inexorable winter.

My father, and then Gentry, mixed with the rain while circumnavigating Old Montreal, and I couldn't help but ponder how Gentry and my father would have walked together in the rain. The past hung in the air like a celestial Chagall, spewing the dust of angels, when I realized what I longed for was a prodigal brother who came home every now and then. I still wonder if, somewhere in the drifting mist, I already knew it was gone—that I might never see again that illumined sanctuary before it was scattered by the dawn.

The next morning, the knock on my office door was immediately followed by Maurice. Sporting a Winchester collar and cuffs, it didn't take much to discern that his normally ebullient countenance was uncharacteristically sober. Dispensing with the pleasantries—save his gratitude for the bottle I had given him—he perfunctorily sat down in the client's chair and solemnly cut to the chase.

"The homeless guy—I did the favor for. Henri . . . quelque chose?"

I nodded.

"And the priest. Was his name Luke 'Ale?"

"Yes," I overreacted.

"Is 'Ale a friend of yours?"

"Yes," I said.

"What's his connection to Cathedral in the Night?"

"What did he do wrong?"

"He didn't do anything wrong."

"So, what did he do right?"

"He got in the way."

"In the way of what?"

"Of your Cathedral Dean," he said.

I got up from my desk and went over to the window. "Beringer?"

"A pretty boy?" he asked.

I wheeled around. "Why the hell would he go after Hale?"

"For the money," Maurice said.

My heart began to race. "Then he picked the wrong pocket."

"If it had been 'Ale's pocket," he replied.

"Whose pocket did he pick?"

"The city's," he imparted.

At first, I didn't believe it.

"I must admit," he said, "for an Anglican priest, he's one helluva businessman!"

"So, what did *you* do?"

"Take it easy, Ben. We're not the villains here."

"We're not?" I shot back. "Then who the fuck is?"

Defensively, he said, "Ask your Dean."

Our firm had been retained to represent the city in contract negotiations to bring the shopping mall and metro stop into the crypt of the Cathedral. Alluding to several "complications" regarding the relevant parties, it appeared that the Dean and diocesan trustees had most of them "worked out." Once I had calmed down and apologized, Maurice set the political table: the Mayor was riding a wave of popularity by "cleaning up" Old Montreal.

"And among the complications," Maurice explained, "was 'Ale's Cathedral in the Night. The Mayor is demanding that the homeless be removed from the streets of the Old City. Though there are vagrancy laws, he can't enforce them without taking political heat—but what he can do is make it difficult for the agencies that support them."

"The church isn't an agency."

"It is if it wants four million a year," Maurice said.

An anvil turned in my gut. "How did you respond?"

"We represent the city!"

"That's a hell of an excuse. Who are the players?"

"The usual suspects," Maurice said. "Developers, the Mayor—and your Cathedral Dean."

"What's Beringer's part?" I fumed.

"What isn't his part? Beringer's the closer! He's in as deep as anyone! Christ," he went on, "he even got the city to build him granite sidewalks!"

"Who's doing the dirty work?"

"Beringer said that he would take care of it."

"What about the Bishop?"

He looked at me—confused. "Don't tell me there's another complication."

"I don't give a fuck about complications. Fuck the complications!"

"I'm sorry, Ben," he said. "It's goddam disappointing. I should know— I'm Catholic! From embezzlement to choir boys, it should be no surprise that most of us gave up on the church."

"I thought at least the church had principles," I said.

Maurice looked almost sympathetic. "A principle's a principle until it costs you money."

"No," I said. "*When* it costs you money."

"In your church," he inquired, "is the Cathedral Dean the predecessor to the Bishop?"

"Not necessarily."

"Can a Dean become a Bishop?"

"Why?" I anxiously came back.

"If your Dean is as good at church politics as he is at the bargaining table, then the current Bishop, whoever he is, is probably a dead man walking."

When Maurice left my office, I picked up the phone and called Christ Church Cathedral. Hearing my name, Beringer's assistant asked me to hold the line. She returned to the phone to say the Dean was occupied, and she would have to get back to me.

I didn't sleep that night, or for the rest of a deafening week of unanswered calls. What kept me awake was less my aversion to Beringer himself, than the truth that I had lived my life by the same self-serving motivations. If there was anything redeeming about the legal game, it was the absence of ethical pretension—which the church, for all its self-righteous indignation, seemed to be unable to admit.

# 26

As I SAT AT the back of Christ Church Cathedral for the Sunday morning service, I felt as though I was suddenly part of a dark and sinister circus. Parishioners I vaguely recognized from my evening Westmount rambles filed fragrantly past, incensing the air with the chance at a morning migraine. Listening to the florid organ noodling in the front of the nave gave me to marvel that the church's demise hadn't happened sooner.

As someone who had never paid much attention, it was the reading that got my goat. While the Deacon was processing the Gospel book high above his head, I could have guessed "The Widow's Mite" was about to be read. A surreptitious check on the appointed passage, as recorded in the back of the Prayer Book, confirmed a lectionary sleight of hand, to the benefit of the preacher.

Following the reading, the Dean embarked on: "Rebuilding Christ's Cathedral." His dulcet delivery magically transformed the pedestrian elements: money, a metro stop, a gleaming office tower—complete with underground shopping. I thought how, if anyone could justify a mall in the exalted name of God, it would have to be someone of Beringer's skill, and wide-eyed eloquence.

I wasn't disappointed. Orating from the pulpit, Beringer's voice dramatically rose and fell as he peered, misty-eyed, at his fawning congregation, and spoke about "sustainability." If it was harder for a rich man to pass through the eye of a needle than to enter God's Kingdom, one would have had to search the sanctuary for a thirty-foot sewing instrument.

As I prepared to confront the triumphant Dean who was happily chatting in the narthex, I managed to endure several young urban professionals chortling behind me. Trapped in enemy territory, it was not for feeling different; I felt trapped because, for all my own high-handed pretensions, I didn't feel different enough. When I entered the narthex, Beringer cast a sidelong glance in my direction—appearing to intensify his earnest grip on an arthritic parishioner.

"Ben, how are you!" he attacked my hand. "Where the heck have you been?"

"I was about to ask you the same question," I said.

"I'm sure you can imagine!"

"Did you get my calls?"

"Yes, I think I did!"

"I'd like to meet with you," I said.

"Just call my assistant!"

"I already have. Several times," I said.

"Though unless it's an emergency," he chummily rejoined, "it will probably have to wait."

"It's an emergency."

"I'm sorry to hear it. Then do, call my assistant!"

"I'll see you tomorrow at five," I said.

"I'm afraid Monday's my day off."

"It's a legal matter."

"Fair enough!" he said. "I look forward to seeing you at five!"

The truth is, I expected him not to show up. Though my hunch that Beringer was conflict-averse proved to be accurate, I underestimated his ability to head me off at the pass. As his assistant motioned me toward his door—which looked deliberately ajar—a bellow from the office prepared me for the fact that this was not going to be a private meeting.

Seeing me, Beringer athletically jumped up and charged across the room. "Welcome!" he declared, gesturing to the empty chair facing the stranger. "Meet the new chancellor of the diocese—" he said, "and college classmate, Tom Hollingsworth!"

"Friends call me Tommy," Hollingsworth smiled.

"Nice to meet you, Tom," I said.

Taking my seat, I noted that Tommy had chosen the comfortable chair. Affably overweight, his jovial grin stretched beneath a walrus moustache. A mop of curly hair, suggesting confusion, attested to the special dispensation granted men who got away with being "eccentric" because they didn't have to make a living.

"I asked Tommy to sit in," Beringer began, "because you mentioned a legal matter." When he enunciated "legal," I was sure a glint of gold flashed out of the side of his mouth. As he leaned back on his desk, I felt myself submitting to the height of Beringer's collar—while trying to suppress the irrepressible image of the Dean wearing it to bed.

"Ben," Beringer graciously went on, "I understand that Stephen is your friend."

"Stephen is the Bishop."

"I'm aware of that," he responded with impressive restraint. "You know how I admire him."

"No, I don't," I said.

"But we're living in a different world. Stephen comes from an enviable time—but I'm charged with the Cathedral's survival."

"Which cathedral is that?"

"Which cathedral?" he inquired. "In a diocese, there's only one cathedral."

"You're being too hard on yourself," I replied. "You have a cathedral, too."

"You're not helping his cause," he seethed.

"Neither are you," I said.

"The church is not a hospital," Beringer retorted.

"It's not?" I impatiently came back.

I had finally managed to offend the Dean. Composing himself, he assumed another tack. "On a plane, someone has to take the oxygen before he can give it to others."

"As long as there's enough to go around," I said.

"In God, there is always enough."

"What about in Jesus?"

"I didn't know there was a difference."

"One of them was homeless," I said.

"This meeting is over," Beringer snapped.

"So, it's about politics," I said.

"Ignore them at your peril."

"That's what Jesus did."

"And look where it got him!" he ignited.

I could see he regretted this last combustion before it came out of his mouth. I even glimpsed Tommy flinch at this breach of theological etiquette. Yet without missing a beat, Beringer crooned, "Which is why he had to die for our sins."

"The Doctrine of Atonement" to which Beringer alluded had always seemed to me a colossal excuse for not having to live the life that Jesus did.

If Jesus died for our sins, and spared us from taking the hit he had to take on the cross, why would he deny us the ultimate glory of taking the hit ourselves? Yet whatever the take—the cross as spectator sport or ultimate way to live one's life—given the Chancellor's oblivious grin, it clearly worked for Tommy.

"Is this priest even a Christian?" Tommy asked—betraying a prior conversation.

The Dean looked embarrassed.

"Which priest?" I demanded.

"The shaman from the jungle!" Tommy said.

I looked at Beringer, now fully flushed, who decided to go for my throat. "How would you answer that?" he said.

"I'm not sure what a Christian is."

"The word 'Christian,'" he ignored my sarcastic reply, "was a pejorative term used by Romans for the dissident followers of Jesus."

"If Christians are dissidents," I couldn't help myself, "I suspect the two of you are safe."

On the strength of my insult, Beringer came clean: "Hale has unorthodox ideas."

"So, that's what this is about," I said. "A witch hunt, to cover for the witches."

The Dean looked gratified by my mounting anger. "Postmodernism notwithstanding," he said, "church doctrine is church doctrine."

"Would you call Hale a heretic?"

Consulting his chin, he rejoined, "Your term, not mine."

Tommy appeared to be utterly confounded by this unnecessary distraction. I guessed he had thought that with encouragement I could be brought into the club; but thanks to my stubbornness, I'd put him in the awkward position of becoming a lawyer. So, with a fretful look—which I had used a hundred times in court to undermine the opposition—Hollingsworth invoked the Trustees' right to take the fiduciary action.

Despite the ammunition I'd been loading for days, I realized I no longer had a target. As much as I might blame him for his mercenary ways, the truth was that Beringer's sin was submitting to a system of jealousy and greed that was dooming a whole generation. As with every institution, the church could not abide the subversive likes of Hale, and I was naïve to think it would be any different in a time of spectacular decline.

As thankful as I was that heretics like Hale no longer met with execution, I nonetheless lamented the passing of the days when beliefs were of greatest consequence. Like Pavlov's dog, the institutional church had done the world's moral bidding, selling itself down a river of regret, rather than going for the sea. If for the Catholic Church, the path of least resistance was excommunication, Anglicans invited heretics for cocktails to make clear who was staying for dinner.

"So, what are you going to do?" I demanded.

"Do about what?" he asked.

"I think you've answered my question," I said.

"It's out of my hands!" he said.

Unable to endure another spineless plea, I said, "There's already blood on them."

Feeling sick, I tried to get up. Having failed the test, I eased back down into my second-rate chair, and queasily peered above our heads at the old-world Victorian ceiling. The elegant coffers looked to be moving—crisscrossing in the room—before I managed to unsteadily stand and make my way across the office.

When I got to the door, I turned and leaned against the mahogany jamb. The two of them were watching with apparent concern, perhaps less for me than for the carpet. As I looked back, there was something pathetic—pathetic about the three of us—making me realize that the game was over, and I had to walk away from the table.

"It's a dark game you're playing," I managed to rail—as Beringer sat motionless. Even in my delirious state, I could see that he knew I meant it, and that as much as he wanted to defend himself, that it wasn't worth the candle. He probably would have been right to dismiss a delirious heretic like me, had it not been that delirium sometimes communicates the truth.

# 27

I WONDER WHAT IT is about the human heart that knows the truth, to deny it, and bets its feigned successes on a game forever fixed by the house of mortality. Perhaps for fear, or for laziness, we shrink from the lives we could have lived, and default to empty measurements of worldly legacy to prove that they were lives worth living. If, as I suspect, in the end we will be judged by how we face our insignificance, the shooting star to which we hitched the wagon of our hopes will burn the trail of our accomplishments.

In this frame of mind, I began to entertain a wholly different future. What was to have been three days in Toronto became two weeks, coast to coast; and like every lonely exile, this one wandered across a desert of regret. If, as my father liked to say, I was a prisoner of hope, and so risked an unending sentence, as I wistfully sifted the mists that drift in the evening streets of Vancouver, I felt as though I was searching for a light that I knew was already gone.

It was there that I received a telephone call from one of the senior partners. As unspecified as my deployment had been, I had probably assumed that my tour would end with a Montreal spring and return me to Boston in summer. But due to retirements, some modest success, and perhaps what he had eaten for breakfast, he tendered an offer of junior partner, and the chance to be home by Christmas.

Anticipating my mother's joy, and my father's understated approval—and the inevitable cacophony of accolades from undoubtedly envious peers—I was mildly surprised by a sense of despair that suddenly burgeoned in my gut as I pondered the move, the short-term logistics, and the long-term implications. Though I had harbored the goal of making partner from the day I joined the firm, as my father had long been given to advise: "Be careful what you wish for." Expressing my utmost gratitude for this gainful recognition, I was given a week to accept what the firm considered a formality.

I thought of an erstwhile college friend whom I first met through Earlie. Ollie had climbed through the ranks of the largest ad agency in the world—where at first he was happy, had a lot of money, and a house in Westchester County. But five years into a stellar career he managed to lose everything: his happiness, his wife, his children, his house, and friends who claimed he had lost his mind.

When Ollie called to tell me what had happened, I began going down to see him. The first time I entered his hospital room, I wasn't even sure it was Ollie: he was pale as hell, and shaking his head as though he had done something wrong. When I asked what was the problem, he kept shaking his head as if nothing could be done—before allowing me how he came unraveled after a business trip to India.

He hazily explained that he was in Bombay with his brand team doing market research. As he stared out the window of the hospital, for the first time Ollie smiled. Vaguely recounting how, with money flowing in and western markets expanding, his client was planning to introduce Vicks Vapo-Rub to the country.

Then, as if something came over him, his eyes became eerily clear as he vividly described being dropped off on a roadside outside the city. The only way into the squalid slum was through eight-foot piles of garbage, which he watched being devoured by hungry dogs at the edge of the shanty town. Making their way along open sewers, with his assistants in their alligator shoes, he caught his first glimpse of the waiting family they were scheduled to interview.

The Manhattan invaders were welcomed by the mother into the ten-by-twelve-foot space. Absent was the father, who was working his shift in a toxic pesticides plant. Served biscuits and tea on the earthen floor by a woman "who looked like she was starving," Ollie surveyed a single hotplate, several bedrolls, and the doorway to a public bathroom.

In response to the routine demographic questions, the mother elatedly explained how blessed she was to have three perfect children: one of them, clearly disabled. She had a wonderful husband with a job, who didn't beat her. When Ollie asked about her "greatest aspiration," she pointed to another corner—containing a decrepit sewing machine in obvious disrepair—and she described how she hoped one day to start a business making women's dresses in order to enable her family of five to move into a larger dwelling.

It was then that Ollie's face screwed up—and he started bawling like a baby. I assumed that something disastrous had happened before he left the shanty. Looking at me, as though he were about to admit to some egregious sin, he managed to wheeze: "I've never felt that grateful in all my life!"

As I was flying back to Montreal on the wings of my professional achievement, I recalled the joke about the airline pilot who gets on the intercom. Engulfed in clouds, he announces that he has some good news and some bad news. "The bad news," he says, "is that we're hopelessly lost. The good news is, we're making great time."

By the time I touched down on the Dorval tarmac, my pitch to Hale was rehearsed. Having banked some healthy reserves, I could afford to work for several years—and depending on how my affairs were handled, probably longer than that. I spent the weekend looking for a place to billet a downsized life, jotting down numbers from real estate signs in the backstreets of Old Montreal.

On Sunday at dusk, I struck out in search of the ephemeral balloon of light. Place d'Armes was empty when I arrived, but with light still in the sky I decided to sit on the cold stone steps in front of the Basilica. Impatiently waiting, as homeless ghosts traipsed across the city square, at last I got up, praying the nomadic cathedral was just around the corner.

Turning onto Jacques Cartier, the Place was as cold as a cauldron. Descending the plaza to the silent river of bygone industry, I made my way to the empty firehouse facing Place d'Youville. And it was then I knew that whatever other venues I happened to pursue, it was over—that even the light in my mind was inexorably extinguished.

It must have been two o'clock in the morning when I found myself on McGregor. I expected to see the manse cast in darkness, but when it came into view I was startled to see the entire house alive with electric light. Fearing that I had happened upon some Gentry family misfortune, I realized I wouldn't be able to sleep and decided not to go home.

As it began to rain, I felt instinctively drawn to the streets of Old Montreal—circling Place d'Armes, then down the swill to the joint where I first met Henri. Enveloped in smoke, I sat at the counter that looked out onto Sainte-Antoine. Ordering coffee, my weary eyes fell to a Montreal Gazette: "Anglican Bishop Resigns" was the headline—with an archived photo of Gentry.

From the dated image, I surmised that the story had been an overnight break. There he was—in pointalist ink, that made him look like he had weathered a war—eternally young, in a boyish sort of way that defied the man he had become. Scrutinizing his cocksure face, I fixed on his wily eyes; in the absence of glasses, his countenance seemed unsettlingly familiar.

I imagined that beneath his solid shoulders stood a tough, wiry physique that would have served him well in the rivers of New Brunswick, or the forests of the Amazon. It was then—like the clichéd deer in headlights—that I was unutterably stunned. Absorbing the shock amidst the cigarettes and dregs, where I had sat with him across the table, I wondered how, for all my touted intuition, I ever could have missed it.

# 28

IT WAS LATE AFTERNOON the following day when I was able to call Gentry's office. Artfully unhelpful, his secretary simply imparted that the Bishop was "out," and in response to my persistence, automatically suggested that I try the University Club. As I entered the Club, and the happy recollection of the first time we met for a drink—where I had watched him presiding with the kings of Montreal as though he owned the place—the once deferential Maître D', who once followed the Bishop, taking notes, quizzically peered as if trying to remember whom I was talking about.

Approaching the Ritz, the headlights of a classic Bentley Continental were shooting diamonds through the air as a white-gloved doorman tipped his hat to greet me. Transfixed by the glittering flumes of light, I thanked him all the same, then forded streams of taillights, flowing down the street and disappearing in the night.

Trekking up Simpson to McGregor Avenue, the manse was returned to darkness. I had already guessed he wasn't there, and instinctively knew where to go. Climbing up to the Oratorio, floating somewhere in the snow, it was hard to fathom that I had met Gentry only fifteen months ago.

It was then that I glimpsed a limning silhouette, turning in the falling snow. At once austere and intimidating, it looked as vulnerable as a boy. I awaited a familiar salutation, but the salutation never came.

"You must like heavy weather!" I called.

The silhouette was silent.

"I'm sorry—about the resignation!" I said.

Still, came no response.

Arriving on the walk where he was standing, I asked: "Where will you go?"

"Nova Scotia," he said.

"What about Hale?"

"His own way—as always," Gentry said.

"He must be happy knowing you're returning to the water."

"My house is on the ocean. Luke once said that riverbanks are poor, and seashores tend to be rich—and that few of us are willing to pay the price . . . before we get to the sea."

"Why did you go into it?" I vengefully came back.

Gentry peered into the distance. "The last time my family wasn't Anglican was before the Reformation. In a family with two sons, one went to the army and the other went into the church."

"It was your brother, wasn't it?" I said at last.

He looked at me as though he'd seen a ghost.

"The man you met here at the Oratorio. It was your brother, wasn't it?" I said.

I feared he would resent the interrogation, but somehow he looked relieved.

"Yes," he said, his eyes fixed on me. "It was my younger brother."

In spite of adolescent boyhood dreams of clandestine espionage, I instantly lost all fascination for international intrigue. All I could see was the tragedy drawn on Gentry's weather-beaten face. I wondered if, for all the certain adulation the two of them must have known, what he may have missed was the possibility that even they were meant to die.

"The Cold War was a dirty, violent, bloody business. And my brother was as noble as there was."

My heart was already rapping in my throat.

"Have you ever heard of the Cambridge 5?"

I told him that I hadn't.

"This one might as well have been one of them—a traitorous, money-grubbing turncoat. When Lukas figured it out, he told him that he had to confess or face imprisonment. Duncan did confess—but behind the iron curtain. And that was the beginning of the end."

I shuddered. "Why didn't he go to Ottawa?"

Gentry faintly smiled. "Lukas never trusted institutions. For all his own institutional success, he really only trusted friends."

Wincing—either with some kind of pain, or with trying to remember—Gentry held me captive until he was able to tell the rest of the story.

"My father took him fishing one Sunday," he said, "after a Bishop's visitation. Lukas met a boy down at the river—a sweet, underprivileged little kid. His face was always as dirty as his dad's—and his dad worked in the Yorkshire mines.

"Lukas wanted to teach his new friend how to fish. Until he was old enough to go on his own, I brought him every week to that river. It was comical seeing the two of them, chumming across such different classes. But unlike me, my ingenuous brother never seemed to notice."

In that moment I didn't want to hear the rest, but Gentry wanted it over.

"When Duncan grew up, he went into the army, and the two of them stayed in touch. As an officer in intelligence, Lukas oversaw recruitment. With Duncan's record, there was no reason to suspect he wouldn't be a trustworthy agent.

"I should have been the soldier," Gentry breathed. "And my brother should have been the priest."

"Your brother was Luke's father," I filled in the blank.

"My brother was Luke's father," Gentry said.

"Who came up with 'Hale'?"

Gentry smiled again. "The bloody Empire," he said. "Luke was an infant when my brother went in—and that was the end of young Luke Gentry."

"What does he know?"

"When his mother died, I started letting out the line."

"That must have been a shock."

"Have you ever seen him shocked?"

"Did he get that from his father?"

"Luke . . ." he almost proudly reminisced, "Luke is exactly like his father." He turned and looked at me. "Do you have a brother?"

"I'm an only child," I said.

Bearing down on me—as though it really mattered—he said: "You should get one."

A solitary passerby, diminishing below, left us alone on the mountain. The accumulating snow in Gentry's flaxen hair made him looked almost young. And I thought again how Gentry and my steadfast father would have gotten along.

"Before he disappeared, all my brother asked was that I be a good father to Luke. And, brother that he was, he told me what that meant. It meant to remember the poor.

"My brother used to say, the gift of privilege is the ransom that it pays to the poor. 'If you remember the poor,' he used to say to me, 'the rest of life takes care of itself.'"

It was as though our conversation had brought him back to a time he had unwittingly forgotten. As I watched him staring intently down the mountain, I wondered if he believed that if he stood there watching long enough, his brother was sure to appear. I sensed that there was something he had left to say, and I left him looking into the distance.

"'The only thing as sad as a dying child,' he said, ' is watching someone being poor. Because a dying child doesn't choose to die,' Lukas said, 'and no one chooses to be poor.'"

"No one?" I facetiously came back.

Gentry smiled. "Maybe just a few."

# 29

GENTRY'S WIFE WAS IN Nova Scotia, and he planned to be there by Christmas. Explaining that he was in the midst of packing up, and no longer belonged to the Club, he promised to have me over for a drink before he left Montreal. As we were parting on Sherbrooke, I gripped his hand and asked, "Where is he now?"

"He's leaving tonight."

"Just like that?"

"They're changing the locks tomorrow."

"Changing the locks?" I incredulously asked.

"Changing the locks," he said.

When I arrived at the gray stone church on Saint Denis, light was leaking from a second story window. Climbing the steps, to see the door was ajar in the clear December cold, I let myself in and leapt up the stairs onto the hollow landing. As I entered the hall, the formidable pile of sleeping bags was gone; scanning the space, the only sign of life was dying in the fireplace.

Next to Hale's diminutive desk leaned a duffle bag against the cot. Approaching the hearth, it looked as if the fire had been burning for several hours. I deduced the duffle bag as good news or bad—either that Hale was about to return or that he'd left in a sudden crisis—so I sauntered about the voluminous space, wondering what to do next, before undertaking a less than justified military inspection.

Arranged on the desk were two pictures, a letter, and a small leather military Bible. On the front of the Bible, in worn gold leaf, was embossed the name, "Lukas Gentry," beneath a fading image that I recognized as the emblem of the Royal Navy. Across the envelope, in lovely cursive script, was written, "My Beloved Luke"—and what I surmised was the Saint Denis address of the church where I was standing.

In the first photograph, an elated Stephen Gentry—more youthful than he'd looked in the Gazette—was leaning into a jocular embrace of what had to be his younger brother. The priest looked constrained by what I suspected was an uncomfortable clerical collar, while Hale's look-a-like was in uniform, down to his military field boots. I suspected it was taken at a British cathedral following Gentry's ordination, and that the junior "Lukas" Gentry was prouder of his brother than the ordinand was of himself.

In the second, antique photograph, a gritty-looking mariner was sitting next to several hard-assed sailors on a square-rigged military ship. The genes were strong—as clear as it was that the skipper had to be a Gentry. Behind their wily faces, self-consciously posed for what looked like a spontaneous snapshot, was the wheel of the ship on which was inscribed: "Fear God, Boys, But Keep the Powder Dry."

"You never know which fire will be the last of the season!"

I started—and Hale was in the doorway.

"I was just at your place!" he said, as he approached.

"You're a hell of a sleuth," I said.

Hale pointed to the chair, inviting me to sit. Dropping to the cot, he drew out his silver flask from inside his jacket. "I wanted to celebrate our final Communion!" he said, handing me the flask.

Unscrewing the top, I took a nervous sip. "Where are you going?" I asked.

He cryptically peered, taking back the flask.

"Wherever it is, you'll need money."

"I don't need money where I'm going," he said.

He took a drink—his first, and his last.

"You can't survive on spiritual economics!"

He handed me the flask. "This is for you."

It was then I realized he was already gone—that however convincing my plan may have been, it was finally irrelevant. When I held up the flask, he waved it off: "Alcohol's no good in the cold."

"Tell me you're going on vacation," I said.

"I'm going on vacation," he said.

"Tell me you're not going to be homeless," I said.

He appraised my anxiety. "In the forest," he said, "until the oil rigs arrived, there was no such thing as being homeless. Now Waorani warriors wander homeless on their own ancestral lands."

Before I could take in the irony, Hale offhandedly went on: "You don't have to go to the Amazon. For Christ's sake, look at Henri."

"Henri?" I said.

He looked at me—seemingly surprised. "Henri is Chippewa Cree."

Suffering from the embarrassing assumption that only Europeans spoke French, I struggled to reimagine Henri as an indigenous tribal member.

"Subsistence living is a bad thing?" Hale mused. "Who came up with that? Piling up a surplus? In the end, the surplus goes away."

"What choice do we have?" I defensively came back.

He raised an ironic brow. "I know a guy who lived his whole life woefully in debt. And when he died, he lost everything."

If I hadn't been on the edge of despair, I'm sure I would have laughed.

"Western economics is pretty roundabout. We don't want to work, or we're afraid of work, so we pretend to work in an office. Few of us are happy—but we might be if we worked. Getting dirty won't kill you.

"Meanwhile," he went on, "we get a second-rate spiritual fix on Sunday morning. God was a laborer—not 'a carpenter'. Maybe if we worked like Jesus, we wouldn't have to think about going to church."

"Do you think," I asked, "that Cathedral in the Night is the way the church was meant to be?"

He peered at me—as though he had never thought about it. "It is, when it's snowing," he said.

"Where are you going?" I almost implored.

"I think I'll stay the winter."

"And then?"

"Maybe Morocco," he said.

"Morocco?"

"There just has to be a river. These days I barely know the River's even there—whether it's up or down. I haven't fished since I left the Amazon. One day I'd like to get to the Nile."

"You won't find many churches in Morocco," I quipped.

"Nor a lot of snow," he said.

"You could pick up Arabic."

"Possibly an indigenous language," he said.

"Are there many tribes in North Africa?" I asked.

"Some of the Berbers are nomadic."

"I wish these tribal Anglicans would be nomadic."

He appreciated the complaint. "Indigenous warfare is different," he said. "The winners take the losers in."

"Beringer took no prisoners," I said.

"Beringer didn't win," Hale said.

"Are you saying he lost?"

"Neither," he said. "He just moved us further down the river."

"You think I need to get past Beringer," I said.

"You're afraid of Beringer," he said.

"Why is that?" I chafed.

"Because," Hale replied, "you're afraid Beringer is you."

He sensed my panic.

"But, you're not," he said.

"How do you know I'm not?"

He looked at me—as though I knew better than that. "For Christ's sake, Ben—you're my brother!"

"Hale," I said, at the end of my rope, "what the hell made you do it?"

"Made me do what?"

"What the hell made you launch Cathedral in the Night?"

He pondered the question. "I wasn't in Montreal a week when I met a farm worker on the street. It was the dead of winter, he had no work, and his family was back in Mexico. In broken English, he said to me, 'I can take the hunger, I can take the cold. But what I can't take is when I look someone in the eye—and he looks away.'"

Getting up, Hale swept the contents from the desk, and slung the duffle bag over his shoulder. Pointing to the flask, he took the lead across the slanting wooden floor, then turned to survey his makeshift abode and commissary one final time. With that, he slammed the double-pole switch and plunged the hall into darkness—save the ashen glow of the last fire of a season that I missed before it was gone.

As we crossed the threshold onto Rue Marie-Anne, pregnant flakes floated in the air. I wondered how he felt as we descended the stairs out into the winter night. Together we walked half a block east to the backstreet behind Saint Denis, where he dropped the duffle bag in the freshly fallen snow, blanketing the winter street.

Holding up the flask, I said, "I don't deserve this."

"Of course you don't!" he said.

"I can—never pay you back."

"Are you saying, you're grateful?"

"Maybe," I confessed.

"Gratitude," he said, squinting in the snow, "means that you can never pay it back."

As my legendary eight-year-old pirate birthday party flashed through a grown man's mind, I understood why, when the pirates had gone home, I felt like I was going to suffocate. Drowning in an undeserved celebration of the pitiful boy I was, I knew that I would never be able to repay the embarrassment of riches I'd been given. What I didn't know was that I had been set up by the ultimate divine deception—which conceals life as the gift that can never be repaid, and requires only that we receive it.

"Hale!" I demanded—sounding the alarm. "Jesus Christ—you can't just live outside!"

"Who can't live outside?"

"You!" I insisted.

"And what's so special about me?"

In that fleeting, paradoxical moment, I glimpsed the genius of Hale's faith. Unlike the rest of us, who were spending our days trying to prove that we were special, what set Hale apart from our vainglorious lives was his courage to confess that he wasn't. And I wondered if this was the courage of Jesus: a reckless abandonment of fear, which left him no choice but to nakedly embrace the whole of creation as a gift.

"How can you leave Claire?" I dumbfoundedly asked.

"I'll never leave Claire," he said.

He could see I was aghast.

"Any more," he said, "than Claire will ever leave me."

"I couldn't do it," I confessed.

"You'll be able to do it when your love is big enough."

"And when is that?" I asked, utterly bewildered.

"When you know that she will never leave."

"Hale," I said. "I once heard that a friend is someone you would trust to set your piton. When it's your piton or his, hanging from a cliff—it's yours he would choose to set."

He smiled, as though he liked the idea.

"Hale—" I said, across a tightening throat. "I think you would set my piton."

He mischievously grinned. "Thanks," he said. "I'd like to think I would."

"Hale," I said. "I'm not sure—that I would. I'm not sure I would set your piton."

Smiling like the brother I never had, he said, "Maybe not yet."

"Hale," I said to him. "I hope we meet again."

"Where are you headed?" he asked.

"Back to Boston."

He looked unconvinced.

"Maybe—someday to France."

"Where in France?" he asked.

"Céret," I replied.

"Maybe I'll see you in Céret."

I watched as he headed up the alley in the snow with the duffle bag on his back, passing underneath a spill of yellow light pouring from the second-story window. Tracking his field boots, striding through the snow, I wondered where he planned to go—and just before his silhouette dissolved into night, I realized that he didn't know. Standing on the walk where we parted, I knew he was no longer there: vanished in a lost, diasporan darkness, that swept across the urban night.

# 30

MONTREAL WAS LUMINOUS WITH Christmas as I walked the Golden Mile, and passed the perennial Yuletide display festooning the windows of the Ritz. As magnificent a city as Montreal was at this exhilarating time of year, I felt the inevitable festive sadness that wells from the absence of home. Yet beneath these poignant, melancholic yearnings lurked the disquieting truth that the home to which I was hoping to return was no longer what it had been.

The Bishop's house was noticeably dark as I turned onto McGregor. Knocking on Gentry's episcopal door, I feared that I had the wrong night. But hearing the dog, and her master's command, I knew I had gotten it right.

The two enthusiastically greeted me. Gentry's purple shirt, less his collar, had seen the better part of the day. Taking my coat, he invited me into the dimly lit living room, where two wing chairs were covered in sheets in front of a crackling fire.

Stripping the chairs like a flamboyant magician, Gentry went to the solitary sideboard. From my seat, I listened to splashes of Scotch cascading from a decanter. There was an intimidating gun vault in the corner, buttressed by several shotguns—and a bamboo fly rod standing at attention in a pair of girded rubber waders.

"Are those Purdey guns?"

Before retiring to his chair, Gentry handed me a dram. "That one is," he pointed. "A sixteen-gauge, side-by-side Sidelock Ejector. Do you hunt?"

"My father did," I said.

"Though I didn't pay twenty thousand dollars," Gentry said. "I got that from my brother. I was a better fisherman, but Lukas was a better shot."

As he gazed into the fire, the flickering flames reflected on his spectacles. It may have been the shrouded furniture that cloaked the room in regret. Like the burden of absence that hovers above a wake in a funeral parlor, I sensed that Gentry had already left for the rivers of Nova Scotia.

"I used to blame my father for everything he did," he said, out of the blue.

"What did he do?"

"What every father does. He tried and failed," Gentry said.

"I didn't know you could do both."

"I hope you're right," he said.

"Do you have children?" I asked.

"I have Luke," he said.

I looked across at him. "I suspect that would be enough."

Gentry smiled, before he sighed: "And look where it got him . . ."

"Look where it got him," I countered his despair.

"Out in the cold . . . like his father."

The fire spit an ember to the wooden floor, and he left it burning there a moment.

"Humble enterprise, isn't it?" he said. "We're born at the mercy of an undeserved past, and we die at the mercy of its future."

"I will never forget his claim the three of us were God's only son," I remembered.

I could see he was listening.

"That's what you did. You made him feel like an only son."

With tears in his eyes, Gentry got up and kicked the coal onto the hearth. "Are you returning to Boston?"

"Yes," I said. "I'm going back to Boston."

"Are you going home?" he unexpectedly asked.

"I'm not sure," I said. "Are you?"

Transfixed by the light of the dying fire, he said, "I'm going home."

"How will I know when I've gotten there?" I asked.

He said into the fire, "You'll just know."

"I take it, home is no longer the church."

Gentry didn't resist. "These days," he said, with unexpected gratitude, "these days I find God in the rivers."

"Beringer once said that there was no better job than being a Cathedral Dean."

Gentry grinned. "The only thing rarer than a priest who is ordained without hopes of becoming a Bishop, is a Bishop who admits to the rest of the world that he really wanted the job."

"You never struck me as ambitious," I said.

"I didn't have to be," Gentry said. "I belonged to the club."

"I didn't know there was a club."

"You only know it when you're not a member."

"You must have taught your nephew not to be a member."

"That would have been the end of the club!"

As I watched him staring into the fire, I wondered if he saw his own Inferno.

"It must be disappointing," I said, attempting a layman's consolation.

"The church is a jealous institution," he said. "And the clergy eat too much."

On both counts, I decided not to tell him I had noticed.

"Beware of priests . . ." he admonished the fire, "who need the church more than the church needs them."

With that, he went over to the gun vault in the corner and returned with a long black tube. "Most American rods are rubbish these days. This one comes from your home state. Thomas & Thomas made a damn good rod. I expect you to be using it in France."

My show of gratitude, however genuine, was summarily dismissed.

"You make France sound like a done deal," I said. "I'm headed back to Boston."

"So, I've heard," he ignored my appeal.

"He asked me where I was going."

Gentry looked at me. "What did you say?"

"That someday I might go to France."

"Did you tell him where?"

"I told him, Céret."

"And what did he say?" he pursued me.

"He said that he would see me in Céret," I said.

Gentry burst into laughter.

"I doubt he could ever find me," I said.

"Oh, he'll find you!" Gentry said. "Several years ago, I was hunting in South Africa when a childhood chum up and died. His son called to ask if I would do the funeral, and my wife explained I couldn't be reached. Luke happened to be there, and bet her he could find me—despite my being incommunicado. Three days later, I was looking through the crosshairs at my nephew in the African savanna. If Luke could find me in a game preserve the size of Israel, I have little doubt he'll be able to find you in a French village called Céret!"

After an hour of regaling him again with descriptions of the Vallespir, I managed to exact the promise of a visit the next time I happened to be there. Taking down my address against a highboy in the hall, he scribbled his and handed it to me. We walked out together to the iron gate, where I shook his hand a final time.

"Don't be surprised if you see me on your terrace."

"I can only hope," I said.

"Faith is the substance of things hoped for," Gentry said, "and evidence of things not seen."

Halfway down McGregor, I turned to see him standing like a sentry in the night. A garbled call resounded down the empty street, as I watched his arm arcing in the dusk. And turning away, I already knew that one day I'd return to Céret, as "Call me when you get there!" continued to ring, if only in my imagination.

# 3 1

As I was cleaning out my office, I felt disconcerted by how little I was leaving behind—and then, by the question of what I had accomplished that would ever be remembered as mine. My once familiar townhouse could have shrugged its shoulders on hearing that I was leaving, having seen my likes many times before, and certain to see my likes again. With my closet of suits already gone, I had only to clasp my briefcase and venture down to Place Ville Marie to bid my colleagues goodbye.

Of course it was Maurice who offered his office to celebrate my final "Salut." As he went to the cabinet, he seemed genuinely sorry to face the fact that I was leaving. But pouring the swansong single malt Scotch, he effusively turned around—raising his glass with an impish grin, to bid me a rapid return.

"At least to Montreal!" he revised his toast, signaling a seat on the sofa.

"What does that mean?"

"If not to practicing the law!" he facetiously came back.

"Reports of my death are exaggerated," I said, peering over my glass.

"I don't believe they are."

"When did I die?"

"When I told you about Beringer," he said.

Startled by the insight, I sweated out his verdict.

"Ever since, you seemed—distracted."

"Distracted from what?"

"From winning," he said.

"Are you calling me lazy?"

Maurice laughed. "You're a goddam workhorse! After you found out about Beringer," he said, "it was as if it didn't matter anymore."

Observing my colleague—and unlikely friend I was suddenly leaving behind—I wondered if he wished for something in his life that he believed

125

he could no longer afford. I wondered if, like me, he had surrendered to regret rather than to losing what he had. I even wondered if he knew the anxiety I knew when I would go to bed at night, only to be tossed by the fear of having lost that wakens men at three in the morning.

"What happens when you realize there's no way left to win?"

"Sacrilege!" Maurice retorted. "What the hell is left?"

"You tell me," I said.

"Family—family and friends."

"Who are these friends?" I asked him.

Embarrassed, Maurice winked: "I'm still working on that!"

"What about the guys on Saint Catherine Street?"

"Probably the best friends I've got!"

I thought of Ollie lying in his sterile room in that lonely psychiatric ward—puzzling over what was so important in my life that I no longer had time for friends. Yet I had to face the truth that it wasn't only friends I had lost like a trail in the night. Having lost my friends, and friends who could have been, I had also lost my self.

"Are we any different from Beringer?" I asked.

"We're lawyers, and Beringer's a priest."

"What's the difference?"

He looked me in the eye. "His reading glasses," Maurice said.

I guffawed. "That's it?"

"What else?" Maurice wheezed, with irrepressible mischief. "Horn-rimmed, tortoiseshell, round, rimless spectacles! Beringer's running for something!"

When our laughter had subsided, Maurice looked at me. "What happened to your friend—Luke 'Ale?"

"Gone," I replied. "But not forgotten."

"I had a part in that."

"We all did," I concurred.

Maurice shook his head. "No," he said, "somehow you were different."

"How the hell is that?"

"You could have been a priest."

I laughed. "If it weren't for the church!"

"But there has to be a church not to go to!" he countered.

"A church with no parishioners!" I said.

"The Catholic Church!" he said.

"I wouldn't have lasted."

"Neither did Jesus," Maurice said.

I scrutinized my colleague. "Do you think . . ." I pondered, "do you think the poor are lazy?"

My friend looked back at me as though he thought I was crazy.

"I hear it all the time!" I insisted.

"But you're not stupid!" Maurice said, not giving an inch. "Imagine sleeping in the cold every night—and collecting soda cans all day long. Being poor is hard work! These assholes throwing stones don't know what they're talking about!"

If I learned anything in these months, it was that friendship comes by the damnedest people. Being "like-minded" had nothing to do with what made Maurice a friend. From a cynic like Maurice, his drive-by ordination was no less than a compliment; and from a right-wing conservative, his take on poverty, a crack in my liberal foundation.

Throwing back the last of my Scotch, I told him I had to go. His concentrated eyes fixed on me. "Ale may have been right," Maurice said. "It never should have been an institution."

"I'll see you," I bade him farewell at the door.

"See you in church," Maurice said.

"I mean it," I told him. "I'll see you again."

He smiled. "That's what I'm afraid of."

Wheeling on the pedestal of Place Ville Marie, and scanning that monumental mountain, I beheld the skyline of a city I had loved and knew would never be my home. Though I had planned to embark on a last nostalgic tour in hopes of seeing Claire, I turned and headed north because I knew it was over, save perhaps the crying, or a prayer. With the winter sun slanting through the biosphere onto this terrestrial zenith—shimmering through space until it found its destined place on the glimmering towers atop the world—I considered once again the possibility that destiny comes by accident: some magnetic intention through the minefields of a life which draws us toward creation's fulfillment.

Wherever Claire had gone, wherever Hale might be, wherever Gentry was in that moment, it was as if the whole city, in a twinkling alignment, had become one magnificent cathedral. And I realized that beneath these glimmering towers which donned the skies with their extravagance, its ultimate magnificence would never be achieved until its last and lost were first and found. So am I still haunted by the renegade priest I watched disappearing in the snow—to baptize a whole city with an unrequited grace that was waiting to be born again.

# 32

Boston was as charming as it had ever been. Whenever I returned I always presumed it was absence that had made the heart grow fond, but its historical case was far too compelling to be written off as deprivation. Back Bay, and Beacon Hill where I grew up, painted a colonial world that would convince the most ardent postmodern critic of the value of history.

It was the town that didn't have to grow up, eternally renewed as it was by faithful schools of freshmen washed onto its shores by the perennial academic tide. I guessed this was why so many like me barely "commenced" across the Charles—dismissing the larger world as the oyster Harvard claimed it had bequeathed. On Saturday mornings, as I walked in the sun along the Esplanade, trying to imagine what Hale was doing in the frozen streets of Montreal, I was stretched between the melancholic sadness of a past that I knew was gone, and the promise of a pedestrian future which seemed to bear no promise at all.

After several weeks in my extravagant digs, on loan from an out-of-town partner, the gas lamps on Commonwealth slowly gave way to the harsh light of working days. A stealth internet had already spawned swarms of sidewalk cafés, graced by software geeks, reaping windfall profits for having fled their high school days. Amidst their artsy antics, comfortable jeans, and uncomfortably expensive shoes, trilled the thrilling energy of personal success and unbridled material pursuit.

Finally facing my rolodex, and the truth of my social life, I sifted through traces of past acquaintances whom I thought might withstand a renewal. Many were lawyers, some were physicians, and the rest were corporate men—vaguely disappointed, once the pleasantries had passed, with whatever successes they had won. Increasingly aware of the limits of a life which had been billed for its limitless potential, I began to fear, despite the high cost of the ticket, that this was all there was to the circus.

What troubled me most was that little seemed wrong with the successful lives we were living. Yet neither did much seem especially right. Most who left Boston had gone to Manhattan, then fled as parents to Greenwich—inimically tied to an umbilical cord that was strangling a whole generation.

Every several weeks I had to go to New York. Driving to New Haven, I would take the Metro North with the Fairfield County commuters, who alone justified the English adoption of the French adjective, "blasé." Nothing around them—in the train, through the window, across the Connecticut landscape—was able to arouse the least surprise beyond their irreproachable lives.

Enfolded in the *Wall Street Journal* or the *Times*, there was no need of a larger world, except to vindicate the unsurpassed successes they believed they had achieved. I wondered how many times they'd ridden together as suits on the 7:08, and never dared to smile, except perhaps to say, "You would be lucky to be someone like me." Disembarking as one and charging up the ramp onto the concourse of Grand Central Station—mechanically dumping the news in platoons of barrels standing at attention—I suddenly feared that what I was discharging was a last opportunity to make more of my life than an obituary, yellowing in yesterday's paper.

It was then that I thought of Ollie again. Calling on the alumni network, I discovered he'd moved back to Cambridge, and was working at an elementary afterschool just across the river. He couldn't have been happier to get my call, and at the end of the week we were sitting in a bistro in Harvard Square, shamelessly reminiscing.

I remember how different Ollie appeared—though not as I would have expected. There was a quiet, irenic sheen in his eyes I never saw in college. If Ollie was born a sensitive soul, I realized what was gone was the unspoken fear that none of us knew had been consuming us all.

"Did you ever go back to India?" I asked.

"I did," he softly replied. "Yeah . . . to a Buddhist monastery. Just after your last visit."

"I'm sorry," I said, "that I lost touch."

"No need. I did too."

"Did you ever see that woman again?"

He didn't miss a beat. "I did! Yeah . . . before my retreat I took a detour to Bombay."

His lingering smile gave way to a grin—as if he were laughing at himself. "I brought her a sewing machine," he said. "It was a little heavy in the backpack.

"Yeah . . ." he reflected, serenely beaming, "my mother's old Singer—barely used.

"Devi was happy. Really . . . really happy. What about you, Ben. Are you happy?"

"I'm successful," I said.

"Ah," he said, ingenuously smiling.

"Are you happy?" I asked him.

"I think so . . ." he said. "Yeah . . . I have to say I'm happy."

"What's the secret?"

"I don't know," he said. "I guess, just . . . giving it up."

"I'm not sure I can."

"I think you can," he said.

"I have a past to contend with."

"Yeah . . ." he said. "Don't we all?"

"Do you ever hear from Earlie?"

"I do hear from him. He asks about you," Ollie said.

"What's he doing?"

"He's working at the Southern Law Poverty Center," he said.

"Earlie went home."

"He did," Ollie smiled. "Yeah . . . Earlie went home."

"Will you remember me to him?"

"I will," Ollie said. "These days we have to stick together."

"Do you miss—the stuff?" I curiously asked.

"Not the excess," he said. He quietly nodded. "But a sewing machine . . . can change a person's life.

"In my mother's closet, it didn't mean a thing. But to that family . . . it meant everything. Though . . . having the nicest sewing machine? Yeah, it works for a while. But there seems to come a time—at least it did for me . . . when it just stops working."

"Who would have thought a sewing machine could change a person's life?"

"Or the lives of her children. Who knows," he reflected, "maybe her children's children . . ."

"How are yours?" I asked him.

"Well!" he replied, returning from his virtual Bombay. "Not as proud of me as they are of their stepdad. But yeah . . . I don't mind."

"Do you think—that we were just afraid?" I asked. "That we were just afraid in college?"

Ollie smiled again. "If Harvard taught me anything, it was how to be afraid."

Crossing Memorial Bridge back to Boston with Ollie's address in my pocket, I felt suddenly compelled to purge the sartorial excesses from my closet. The moment I returned I was throwing three-piece suits onto the four-poster bed. Stuffing them in bags, I went down to the Salvation Army on Washington Street, and cathartically departed as though I'd been relieved of a sack of yesterday's dreams.

Still receiving packets of second-class mail being forwarded from Montreal, I have to admit that I followed the Christ Church Cathedral communiqués with interest. It was early spring when the envelope came from "The Bishop's Nominating Committee," conveying the process required to elect "The Ninth Bishop of Montreal." An elaborate brochure outlining the details of the "Nominee Walkabouts," described what I could only imagine as a clerical beauty pageant.

The Nominating Committee recognized itself for its "hard and diligent work" that had produced the slate of candidates it was "privileged to present." At the top of the list—ostensibly for reason of alphabetical order—was "John Robert Beringer," accompanied by his handsome, diffident visage. All the episcopal nominees possessed the predictable credentials: significant degrees, committee memberships, and "cardinal" rectorships; but none enjoyed the alliterative ring of "Bishop Robert Beringer."

Following the scrolls of elite diplomas came the candidates' personal statements, beginning with Beringer's modest treatise: "Christ's Mission to the World." While in no way did he want to detract from his predecessor's "Godly leadership," he was nonetheless concerned that certain ministries were no longer "sustainable." Though he didn't divulge which ones they were, it was "critical the budget be balanced"—alluding to fiscal oversight as "a gift" he might be able to offer.

As if he almost forgot, Beringer ended by giving thanks to God for the Cathedral's million-dollar revenue stream—of which he was "only a steward." By "a veritable movement of the Holy Spirit," he described "the unlikely alliance between business, the city, and the diocese, in doing God's work together." Introducing a plan to administer grants to "priests in struggling churches," he couldn't have been more optimistic about the future of the diocese.

"I'm no rock star," launched his biography. I guessed this confession wouldn't hurt him. "I'm a monk. A poet. An artist," he confessed. "I ride an old motorcycle." I recalled a picture of a vintage BMW, hanging in his office.

"The last thing I wanted was to be a priest. I guess that's what you get when you say, 'No!' But then I realized it wasn't my choice—and therefore, it had to be God's.

"During most of prep school, I was angry at God. Football had been my passion. All I wanted was to be the quarterback—but God had other plans! Injured as a freshman, I had to face the truth that I would never play again."

Beringer explained it was as a rower that he found his "deeper longing for God." But as a winning middleweight, he also heard God's call for "successful leadership." In conclusion, he allowed how—in the short time he'd been "blessed by the Diocese of Montreal"—he had come to appreciate "its gifted laity," and had "grown to love you all."

Considering Beringer's financial plan to help priests in moribund churches, one would have been naïve to lay down a bet on any other horse but the Dean. Though election was dependent on a majority in both lay and clerical orders, in the Anglican Church, the tail wagged the dog—and the Dean had clearly tamed the latter. Incredulous as I may have been about Beringer's insincerity, I had to admit, as a chess-playing lawyer, I couldn't have done it any better.

# 33

ONE SUNDAY AFTERNOON, AS I was taking a solitary stroll in the Boston Gardens, I came upon a gathering that made me think of Cathedral in the Night. Albeit in the day, and lacking the romance of that memorable plume of light, I approached what looked like the disorganized beginnings of an outdoor worship service. Still yearning to fill the void that had been left in the streets of Old Montreal, I suspect I was drawn to anything remotely resembling Hale's community.

Before I arrived, I was singlehandedly ambushed by a young androgynous priest, who I guessed had identified me from afar as a "reliable" participant. Prematurely entrusted with a Book of Common Prayer, I was drafted to read the Nicene Creed. As one who had always felt alienated by this endless, gymnastic recitation, I could only wonder how it must have sounded to people living on the street.

Desperate as I was to make my escape, I stayed through the end of the service, enduring extravagant British accents I guessed had been honed in Cleveland. As well-meaning as the clergy appeared to be, there was a tonal condescension that ground from the gullet, tremored in the air, and tapered to a lingual trill. And as substantial as Beringer's collar had been, it had nothing on these three athletic socks—whose towering height held me rapt with whether their next breath would be their last.

At the Benediction, I found myself distracted by an African-American man, who was turned out in a Brooks Brothers suit and familiar-looking tie. At first I wasn't sure why the ensemble even caught my attention. But bearing down on his gaberdine lapel, I made out a flag of Quebec—suspiciously like the one by which Maurice had made me a citizen.

Before I could process the coincidence I was overwhelmed by gratitude. For what, I wasn't sure, except for how much better the suit looked on him than on me. Perhaps it was his seeming lack of resentment, or his proud, yet generous comportment, that made me feel indebted to this un-witting heir of my expensive Brooks Brothers suit.

I realize what I wanted by the purging of my closet was more than a temporary balm for the sores of a life that had escaped the injustice which had given me the suit in the first place. As he graciously received his brown bag lunch from one of the well-heeled volunteers—some of whom I guessed were probably lawyers who had retired from the life I was living—I felt both heartened by these dutiful peers thirty years my senior, and petrified that this was the prosaic way my life was going to turn out. Climbing the steps to the enormous apartment on Commonwealth Avenue, all I wanted from my bankrupt life was to somehow feel grateful again.

As I listened to my mother's mellifluous voice on the answering machine, I was puzzled by what sounded like her business-like tone, and played the message again. Inviting me to dinner on Friday night, her usual vivaciousness seemed oddly subdued, inspiring me to pick up the phone to ensure all was well. Apologetic for causing me concern, she allowed how "Dad and I" had something they wanted to ask of me at the house on Bea-con Hill.

I felt almost anxious as I waited for the door to open into the April evening. Already smiling, my father looked grateful I had made the effort to come, and my mother was faithfully at his side in wait of her only child. Kissing my mother on her graceful cheek, and shaking my father's hand, we retreated into the living room, in all its old-shoe glory.

Reviewing the progress of my mother's next book and my father's philanthropic projects, we predictably moved to a cross-examination of my work and social life. With little to report on either front, silence filled the room. Then, in his inimitably forthright way, my father said: "Ben, we're moving to Maine."

The truth is, I'd considered the possibility as Friday evening approached. Though my parents appeared to be no less active than before I left for Mon-treal, even so I sensed they had less in reserve to fuel their demanding lives. If indeed they were graying gracefully, if not at the top of their game, my father had taken his own advice to "leave when they're disappointed."

Nevertheless, York Harbor was comfortably close to their Boston network, and the big summerhouse would generously meet their expecta-tions by the sea. My father described the work to be done on its massive fieldstone foundation, while my mother rattled off renovations required for a year-round life. I confess that as prepared as I thought I was, I felt irrationally cornered—that a decision which was clearly theirs to make had also been made for me.

Beholding the table, meticulously set in typically sterling splendor, I realized how much I loved them both, and that somehow the party was over. As we sat down to dinner, I was suddenly struck by how fragile my family had become. It was after the first course that my mother explained the reason for the invitation: they wanted to offer me their beloved house on Acorn Street.

I remember my father's discerning eyes, quietly fixed on me—giving me license to stand my ground against his parents' wishes. Awash in genuine appreciation, I clumsily attempted to explain how my immediate future was "too uncertain to make such a certain commitment." Though they may have anticipated my resistance to living where I grew up, they were clearly caught off-guard by an answer that called into question my staying in Boston.

"Darling," my mother lovingly implored, "what is it that you want?"

Before I could suppress the irrepressible impulse, I replied: "The house in France!"

My father let go a peal of laughter, and my mother, her salad fork. If at first my uncharacteristic appeal seemed like quixotic longing, my father detected that more was afoot than a superficial distraction. To watch him, one might have assumed it was he who had won the airplane ticket to France—before he extracted a smile from my mother that instantly granted me my wish.

When my father grew silent during dessert, my mother read the table—suggesting we retire to the living room, where she would return with the coffee. As I sat down, my father preempted my mother's caffeinated suggestion, going to the sideboard and pouring two generous snifters of Armagnac. He quietly passed a glass to my hand and sat down in his slip-covered chair, raising his feet onto the ottoman before bearing down on me.

"You're leaving the law," my father said.

I wished he hadn't been a lawyer. "Yes," I confessed.

He continued to stare. "And you're moving to France," he said.

Imprisoned in my chair, I was stricken by the fear that once again I had failed him. His gaze went out the window through the hand-blown glass that blinked onto Acorn Street, and for the first time I sensed that my father's life wasn't all it had seemed. As I sat in wait of his final judgment, he turned and vulnerably smiled—as though, in spite of any disappointment, he was happy for me.

"You never really wanted what I had, did you, Ben?"

The question brought me up short.

"You never wanted to be a lawyer."

"I already told you that."

He raised a brow. "You told me that?"

"I told you what I wanted to be."

He inquisitively stared.

"But it would have been hard to make a living," I said.

"What living was that?"

"For Christ's sake," I said, "Protector of the Animals!"

For the first time in my life, I saw tears in his eyes.

"What did—you want?" I finally asked.

"I wanted to be a physician."

I'd never heard this before.

"I loved biology. I loved the idea—of healing."

"Do you regret having gone into the law?"

He blinked. "I had you instead."

As witness to a man who had played poker so long that I didn't know when he was playing, his deferential son could only have presumed that self-doubt was another man's plight. Free to consider my immortal father as yet another mortal player, I was given to face the possibility that Ben Sr. was only human. I wondered if it was their similar bearing—or that their greatest generation was ending—but in that moment of resignation, I could only think of Stephen Gentry.

"When are you leaving?"

"Yesterday," I said.

He smiled with boyish mischief. "What if we hadn't given you the house?"

"But, you did," I said.

He laughed.

"Do you wish you were coming?" I asked.

"Yes. I wish I were coming."

"Then come!" I said.

He wistfully winced. "That train may have left the station."

I must have looked regretful.

"Don't be," he replied. "There's nothing wrong with a wish."

# 34

Summer flew by on fluttering wings of unbounded anticipation. Days after dinner on Beacon Hill, I broke the news to my colleagues, who earnestly expressed their genuine regret before scrambling to become the next partner. The following weeks were devoted to passing the reins to associates, and as the bright yellow leaves lit the late September trees, I was able to see beyond the Charles.

With my departure approaching, I decided to take a final pilgrimage north. If all we have are memories of the life we have left behind, I felt drawn to the silent river where mine was more than it ever had been. As well as I knew the choices I had made were less than they could have been, I hoped that somewhere, before the river's end, was the chance to make them again.

Not surprisingly, Beringer was elected Bishop on the first ballot. The embossed announcement came in the mail complete with a family portrait, sporting his two sons who were flanking their dad who had made it all possible. I declined the generous offer to contribute to "The Bishop's In-Vestment Fund"—a witty jeu de mot to raise six thousand dollars for Beringer's cope and miter.

Aware as I had been of missing Montreal in the months since I had left, as I crossed the bridge I wasn't prepared for my breath to be taken away. Shimmering in the autumn dark like a transitory curtain of light, I might as well have heard, "Be still my heart," from behind the steering wheel. Like an anxious adolescent, I romantically knew that I had no choice but to go on—as if hoping to recover the traces of a lover who had disappeared in the night.

By the time I parked the car underneath the Ritz I felt like I'd been hit by a train. As much as I was craving the freshly laundered linens awaiting me ten floors north, I decided to leave my suitcase in the car, and emerged from the garage on foot. Heading east on Sherbrooke to Saint Denis, I turned north toward the Plateau—an adventurer searching for a fellow explorer who had been lost by his incompetence.

From the far side of the street, my apprehensive gaze gave way to the gray stone church. I recalled a remark once made by a friend and medical ethicist: "I may not be able to define the term 'death,' but I sure as hell know it when I see it." Unruly weeds shrouded the granite walls, and the red Gothic door was peeling—and in black, helter-skelter, paint-can penmanship was scrawled the inscription, "Dieu est Mort."

Crossing the street, I feared the graffiti artist knew something that I didn't. When I got to the alley, the spectral yellow light still spilled from the second-story window. If I knew Hale was gone, and that nothing I could do would bring back Cathedral in the Night, I felt inexorably drawn down to the river, where it had begun.

At the edge of the Old City I could already see that the Mayor had done his job. In the months since I left, it had already become another man's town at night—an absentee landlord's, for whom its oversight was at best an inconvenience. Row house porticos, and former homes to most of Cathedral in the Night, yawned like hollow men in the somnolent dark and small hours of the morning.

As I descended Saint Laurent, each gloomy doorway swallowed the lingering light, as if breathing in the question: What happens when someone has nowhere to go at night? Just north of Saint-Antoine—above my head, on a stoop strewn with newspaper and shadows—something unexpectedly startled to life next to a small cardboard box. Recovering from the jolt, I climbed the stairs to suspicious eyes, staring out at me.

"Henri?" I gasped.

"Ben?" came a voice.

My heart leapt up the stairs. "Oui! C'est moi!"

Frantically struggling from the swaddle of blankets that enveloped his sleeping bag, he shot up in the air with open arms, as if I were the last man on earth. Wild, unruly hair had grown onto his shoulders, and his grin was down a tooth or two. Yet through the somber darkness, the twinkle in his eyes was proof that it could only be Henri.

Inviting me to sit, he patted the step like the self-appointed Duke of Montreal. Quizzically asking where I had been, I felt ashamed of my unannounced departure. I explained that my work had returned me to

Boston—about which Henri seemed to be intrigued—giving me to realize, for all the months I'd known him, how little I had shared about myself.

When I inquired about his life after Cathedral in the Night, Henri solemnly recounted that, per order of the Mayor, most everyone had gone to the nearby slums of Griffintown. Thanks to a sympathetic cop on the beat—whom Henri knew, "grace à Luke"—he was allowed to sleep in Old Montreal as long as he set up after midnight. Admitting that with Hale's disappearance he regrettably fell off the wagon, Henri assured me that as soon as he got back on his feet, he would never drink again.

It was then that I asked if he had seen Hale, and he looked at me as though he'd seen a ghost. His pleading eyes let go a torrent of tears, and his blistered lips began to quiver. Helpless to console my devastated friend—about what, I didn't know—I put my arm around his trembling, boney shoulders, and anxiously waited it out.

Managing to stand, he retreated to the shadows that filled the dingy portico, and bawling like a baby, emerged from the cavern with a snow-shoe under his arm. Lodged in the binding was Hale's unmistakable British military field boot. "Il est mort!" Henri uncontrollably wept. "Ben—Luke est mort!"

Through his heaving anguish, Henri recalled last year's blizzard that besieged Montreal. He related how everyone living on the street was ordered indoors by the police—but claustrophobic in the crowded shelter, he even left his church behind. When he returned to retrieve his prized possession, he was told someone fitting Hale's description had seen the cardboard church, asked about its owner, and fled out into the night.

Sitting down again, Henri dropped the snowshoe, and then his face, into his hands. "Osti de tabarnak de calice!" he cried. "Osti d'crisse de tabarnak!" Pounding his chest, he chastised a "chasse-neige" before proclaiming it was all his fault—that the reason Hale was dead was not the "chasse-neige," but his selfishness in going outside.

As I sat there with Henri, looking out together onto that desolate street, I hoped for a hoax, then a misunderstanding, and finally a terrible mistake. I wondered if this was what it meant to be in shock. Gripping the cold stone step beneath me, sweat was beading on my brow—dizzy as hell, I had all I could do to endure the suffocating grief.

Before trying to fathom the world without Hale, Henri asked if I was "coming home." I told him I was leaving the United States, and reluctantly disclosed my destination. With a longing gaze, he curiously asked if there were "palmiers"—palm trees—there.

When I confessed that there were, ecstasy welled in his teary, shining eyes. Aware that even in late September, winter was already coming, I asked if he was planning to live in a shelter, or somewhere out on the street. But as we looked out, I guessed what he was seeing were palm trees in the south of France—and then, without the slightest show of resentment, he pronounced: "Je te rendrai visite!"

As much as I wished that somehow he could visit, I was well aware of the odds. Then, getting up from the stoop, he extended his hand, like a host to his parting guest. Gripping my hand, in his terrible English, he declared, "I you prom-eese!"

Halfway down the block, through the dampness of dawn, I heard him cry out: "Ben!" I turned around to see him in the portico, with his hands cupped around his mouth. The best I can do is a rough translation of what he called to me.

"Ben!" he hollered, through a megaphone of fingers. "Do you think you are better than me?"

I remember hesitating—not for lack of an answer, but for having been respected by my name.

"No!" I hollered back, up the sonorous street. "I know that I'm no better than you!"

Seeming satisfied, Henri disappeared back into his portico.

"Henri!" I called to him.

Henri reappeared.

"Do you think that you are better than me?"

He laughed, like a solitary friend in the night. "There is no better!" he said.

"What is there?" I replied.

He threw his arms in the air. "It's all of us together!"

# 35

As THE PITCH OF night curdled toward dawn on the steps of the Basilica, I gazed across that memorable square, through the ghosts of Cathedral in the Night. Skirting Place d'Youville, Place Jacques Cartier, and finally landing there, I knew that he was gone, that he wasn't coming back, and that time had inescapably moved on. I wondered if Hale's minyan had lasted as long as that of the star-crossed apostles; and I wondered how long it would be remembered before the memory was gone.

Dawn was waking the sleeping port and seeping onto Place d'Armes when I resolved that by the time the street lamps were extinguished, I would be up and gone. A light September rain baptized the square with unexpected magnanimity, as if cleansing the sins of a difficult past it would never have to see again. Before I could account for my racing heart, rapping against my throat, I blearily gleaned, as if in a dream, a woman pushing a stroller.

Fifty meters from the steps, she happily looked up as if she'd been expecting me—and relinquishing her charge, leapt up the stairs with ec- statically outstretched arms. If it was hard to fathom any greater joy than holding Claire McWilliams in the flesh, it was harder to imagine any greater pain than embracing her mortality. In that sad embrace, I breathed her fra- grant hair like a pathetically tortured adolescent, and reluctantly releasing her sensual back, wondered how I could leave again.

"You have to meet Luke!" she said, taking my hand and leading me down the steps. Jauntily plucking the infant from the stroller, she proudly presented him to me. Her white, oversized oxford shirt only heightened her femininity, and her voluptuous smile, and joyful, pleading eyes, literally took my breath away.

"Where have you been, Ben Cabot!" she said.

"Boston," I obtusely answered.

"You didn't say goodbye!"

"That way," I repented, "I knew I would have to come back."

She generously smiled.

"He's—handsome," I said.

"He takes after his father!" she said.

"What was that?" I asked.

"He takes after Luke!"

"He—smiles more than his father," I faltered.

Her laughter cascaded down the empty street. "Who doesn't!" she rejoiced.

Playfully tilting her lovely head, she left me speechless with grief. As little Luke limply nodded off to sleep, she cradled him back into the stroller. When she stood back up, she brushed a wisp of hair from the corner of her luscious mouth.

She studied me. "I know Luke died," she said.

I held my breath.

"But he's not dead."

Countering my sympathetic gaze with her utterly unabashed smile, I wanted to believe her almost as much as I wanted her to be happy. Before I could launch an ambiguous response—"It depends on what you mean by death," and so on—it was as though she had already anticipated my heartlessly agnostic reply.

"We wouldn't be standing here, talking," she said, "if Luke weren't alive in this moment."

"In that sense," I allowed.

Claire looked at me, amused. "Is there any other sense?" she asked.

As tenderly as I felt for her—and as desperate not to hurt her as I was—there was nonetheless something in the strength of her gaze which gave me to believe in the question.

"The—physical sense," I attempted a reply.

"What do you mean, physical?" she asked.

"Like Lazarus—being resurrected from the dead."

"I think of that as resuscitation."

"What's the difference?"

She considered the question. "Lazarus died again," she said.

A fall of hair broke onto her slender shoulder. "I see babies die every night," she said. "And I fill out death certificates. But there is never any place to tell who they were—or where it was that they went."

"Do you—" I dislodged the puck in my throat, "do you—know where they went?"

"They never went so far that they couldn't be remembered. They never went so far they were forgotten.

"Sometimes Luke would come to the hospital at night to wait for the end of my shift. He would often go to the pediatric ward to visit the sickest kids. Last winter he met an eight-year-old girl, who was getting ready to die."

"It was snowing," she went on, "so Luke convinced a nurse to let him take the little girl outside. He found a snowsuit, and carried her out onto the lawn to show her how to make a snow angel. Together they made a lawn of angels, before she got too cold to be outside. I'll never forget my colleague's description of the little girl's face. She said it was as though she had undergone a miraculous transformation.

"After she died, Luke kept coming back to visit the lawn of angels. Each time it snowed, he would come to see if he could still make out their traces. Then came the snow when he came to me to say that he couldn't see the traces anymore—and how happy it made him to know she had gone, so that she could always be with us."

Claire gleaned the uncertainty in my eyes.

"Luke once said to me, 'Look at me—and tell me what you see.' And I looked back, lost in his gaze, and told him I saw someone I loved. Then he said to me, 'Now close your eyes—and tell me what you see.' I told him that I saw the Amazon River, and Cathedral in the Night . . . and a solitary past, and a generous heart, and a man who would never give up.

"Then he said to me, 'Now open my eyes,' and he asked which vision was more real. I told him, neither—that they were both real. Just in different ways. And he smiled, as if he were satisfied that at last, I understood."

"What did you understand?"

"That the second way of seeing was no less real than the first."

"Do you still believe it's true?"

"No," she replied. "The second way is more real than the first."

"Why is that?" I asked her.

"Because the second way . . . the second way of seeing has no end."

"Does he talk to you?"

"He smiles at me," she said.

"What do you say—to him?"

She peered at me with mischief. "That his smile is more than he was ever able to say."

She was crying. At first I wanted to reach out to her, but somehow I knew that I couldn't. Eerily transfigured in the morning light, she was meant to stand alone.

"I'm not crying because I miss him," she wept. "I'm crying . . . because he is here."

As often as I'd heard that truth and beauty were one, and dismissed it as an empty maxim, regarding her face in the morning light, I had to believe that it was true.

"So much for scientific evidence," I teased.

"I go where the evidence leads."

"Most scientists wouldn't call that evidence."

"Most churches wouldn't call that God."

"Why not?" I conceded.

"Because they're terrified of anything they can't understand.

"Luke used to quote a Medieval mystic who said, 'God is an infinite sphere whose center is everywhere, and whose circumference is nowhere.' When I asked him what it meant, he said he didn't know, but he was pretty sure it was true."

With that, Claire came forward and kissed me on the cheek. Embracing her body in the middle of Place d'Armes, I felt as if I were going to drown. As much as I wanted to hold her there forever, somehow I found the strength to let her go—hoping it was true that if I let her go, she would be with me forever.

"I loved you, you know," I said to her.

"I know. And I loved you."

"I didn't know," I said.

"You couldn't have," she said.

"Why not?"

"It wasn't love to you."

"What was it?" I asked.

"Possession," she said. "It isn't love until it's given away."

"I feel as though I have dreamed of you my whole life."

She smiled. "Then let me go."

"I'm not sure that I can."

"You have no choice," she said. "If you don't, I can't come back."

At an utter loss, it was all I could do to endure the agony of our parting.

"Luke once said to me, 'God is a river.' And I asked, 'Do you mean God is like a river?' He answered, 'If God were only *like* a river, we would never jump in.'"

"Tell me the river is love," I said.

"I didn't have to tell you," she said.

Retreating on the plaza just to keep her in my view, I knew that she would always be with me. I considered what she said, and what she didn't say: that the transcendent evidence was so ubiquitous that we didn't even notice we were breathing. And I thought of how a little girl, whose name I'd never know, was as real as the air I was breathing—to be borne on angels' wings, rising from the snow, to change the world forever.

Whatever were my doubts as I said goodbye to the woman I would always love—and the fleeting fiery fuses of subversive men like Jesus were being systematically extinguished—when all was said and done, and the story was played out, and it would be all over but the crying, it would be such women, by their pure, transparent faith, who would vouch for what it was that truly happened. Claire's beatific strength came by way of what she didn't say: opening herself to a spectacular transcendence whose nature was to live forever. I wondered if it had to have been a woman to convince a hardened skeptic like me that there might be a way to receive life's vast abundance that transcended taking all that I could get.

# 3 6

I FELT THE DELIRIUM of sleep deprivation overtaking my judgment when I decided to visit the firm a final time to say goodbye to Maurice. Just before eight, I charged Place Ville Marie and shot up to the thirtieth floor. Knocking on his door, I found him alone, already engrossed in work.

Looking up, his stern concentration gave way to instant ebullience, offering a welcoming Quebecois embrace and a seat on the familiar sofa. When he nodded at the espresso machine, I allowed him that nothing would be better, and in minutes we had covered most of what had happened since my leaving Montreal. With that, I marshaled the courage to break the news of my impending move—predictably chased by one of Maurice's relentless cross-examinations.

"Paris?" he asked.

When I didn't reply, he looked at me with suspicion. "You're leaving the law."

"Yes," I said.

"To live in the south of France."

"Yes," I said.

"In your parents' bergerie."

"It's mine, now. But yes," I answered.

He stared at me with disbelief. "What the hell are you going to do?"

"I'm not sure," I said.

He sat down on his desk.

"I won't need much," I told him.

"Someday I'll hear you've become a monk," he said.

"I've had about enough of the church."

"Maybe you expected too much," he said.

"Maybe I expected too little."

"Sometimes, expectations cost too much."

"They never cost too much," I said.

"I wish I had your faith."

"I wish I had your salary."

"No, you don't," Maurice said.

"Do you remember," he reflected, "when you asked about the difference between Beringer—and you and me?"

"You said, his reading glasses."

Maurice laughed.

"Don't tell me it wasn't his glasses."

A cloud momentarily veiled the morning sun that had been filling his corner window.

"I've thought about this—quite a bit," he said.

"And?" I impatiently came back.

"I'm not sure there is much difference," he said.

It wasn't what I wanted to hear.

"The difference lies between Hale—and you and me."

"What happened to Beringer?" I said.

"Beringer is irrelevant," he said.

"So, what's the difference?" I snapped.

He looked me in the eye. "Fear," he said. "Hale had no fear."

As much as I wanted to defend myself, I knew that he was right. We both had been running from fear so long that we no longer knew we were running. In fact our whole generation had been running so long, it didn't know it was running—and in our desperate pursuit of ever greater life, we hadn't even noticed we were dying.

It was not only Beringer who had spent his life fending off impending death. It was all of us, whose anesthetic dreams had drugged the only life worth living. I wanted to tell him that Hale was dead, and even wondered why I didn't—except that, thanks to his unwitting insight, Hale was very much alive.

"What are we afraid of?" I finally said.

"What aren't we afraid of?" Maurice said. "That we aren't good enough. That we'll be outdone. That in the end, we won't have made it."

"How was it that Hale had no fear?" I asked.

"Maybe he knew something that we didn't."

"I used to think . . ." I said, "that all I had to do was to have the right point of view. The trouble is, liberals like me are just as greedy as conservatives like you."

Maurice laughed. "But your conservatives are a very different animal!"

"How are they different?"

"Yours take no prisoners!" Maurice ironically grinned. "Though I have to admit, if nothing else, they have the courage of their convictions!"

"Such as they are."

"Oh, don't get me wrong! I find their selfishness despicable."

Before I was able to feel relieved, Maurice pleasantly went on: "Whereas your liberals, for all their democratic convictions, lack the courage of their own."

"Are you referring to me?"

He looked at me. "Only you can answer that."

"I think you're referring to me," I said.

"I know I'm referring to your Dean."

"I wonder what happened?" I ruminated.

"You liberals became the elite. Now you have too much to protect," he mused. I remember squirming on the sofa. "You used to be part of the fight for justice. Now you just talk about it."

"These days," I reflected, "when I hear that a friend has made a lot of money, it doesn't feel much different from hearing that he's been in a serious car accident."

"Yet we all have to live," Maurice excused us both. "It's a matter of having enough."

"When Rockefeller was asked how much was enough . . ."

Maurice winked. "Just a little bit more."

Bearing down on me, he thoughtfully inquired, "What would be enough . . . for you?"

"To be remembered," I said.

"In a shepherd's cottage . . . in the south of France," he said.

"I didn't say I wanted to be famous," I replied. "I said I wanted to be remembered."

"By whom?" he asked.

"By someone . . ." I said, "by someone who will never know my name."

He seemed to relish the thought. "What ever happened to the homeless guy—with the lease?"

"Henri," I said. "He's back on the street."

"I'm sorry to hear it," Maurice said.

"He needs to be remembered," I said at last.

"He needs to be remembered," Maurice said.

Out of the blue, I asked, "What does '*Osti de tabarnak*' mean?"

He erupted with laughter. "You're either keeping company with derelicts," he said, "or with very religious people! It either means the host of the tabernacle, or the worst of all obscenities! Who said it?"

"A religious derelict," I said.

"Jesus?"

"You never know," I said. "What about *chasse-neige*?"

Puzzled by the question, he said, "*Chasse-neige* is a snowplow."

Sitting there, dangling my empty coffee cup, I felt like I was going to be sick.

"Why do you ask?"

"Have you . . . ever heard of someone being killed by a snowplow?"

"More than once," he said.

"Recently?" I asked.

"I recall a case last winter. A driver thought he saw a body fall from his truck as he was emptying snow at the dump. But when he returned with the Mounted Police, nothing was ever found."

Maurice's assistant appeared at the door to remind him of a nine o'clock appointment. Finding my sea-legs, I slowly got up and followed him out into the hall.

"Remember me," he said, gripping my hand.

"I'll be seeing you," I said.

"I hope so!" Maurice cordially rejoined.

"I mean it," I challenged his decorum.

"Maybe you're just braver than I," he said.

"Or stupider," I said.

"There's a difference?" Maurice asked.

"Then come and be stupid," I said.

"Maybe someday," he might as well have sighed.

"But someday never comes," I said.

# 37

HAVING BEEN UP FOR twenty-four hours, I wasn't at my best. I probably should have passed on the chance that was waiting to come to fruition. Tempting fate because it was there, I felt inevitably drawn to what I once presumed to be a sacred place, and now perceived as the scene of a crime.

Union Square was gridlocked with the morning commute in front of Christ Church Cathedral. Shrouded in scaffolds and rung by a maze of temporary walks, pile drivers and jackhammers relentlessly pummeled the earth and surrounding pavement. Like dinosaurs, colossal excavators dwarfed passing pedestrians—frantically digging in the valuable dirt as though something had been lost.

Looking skyward at the skeletal girders soaring forty floors in the air, it was hard to make out the Cathedral spire against the cruciform grid. I couldn't help but think of Gentry's conviction that "no man can serve two masters." Yet whether by history, or Beringer himself, an end was surely coming.

A forest green Rover traversed the walk and entered the construction zone. Before he emerged from behind the wheel, my heart was already pounding. Perhaps by uncanny accident, he glanced down to where I stood—as if to confirm, by royal double-take, some paranoid, visceral suspicion.

At first I thought he was going to feign not knowing who I was. Consumed by rage, I stormed the fence and went straight for the newly minted Bishop. Seemingly oblivious, Beringer extended a gracious, welcoming hand.

"Ben!" he said. "Well, how are you?"

"Hale is dead," I said.

"What was that?"

"Hale is dead."

"The priest of Cathedral in the Night? My God! I'm sorry to hear it!" he said. "Wasn't he a friend of yours?"

"He died on the street—in a snowstorm," I said.

"That's tragic!" Beringer replied.

"It happens every day."

"I'm aware of that. We support a homeless shelter."

"Are you selling tickets?"

He looked confused.

"To keep the homeless out of the Cathedral."

"What does that mean?"

"The way you did in Boston. At your church in Copley Square."

Flushed with anger, he turned his back and opened the rear door of the Rover. Retrieving a handsome belting leather briefcase, he closed the door and locked it. "Well, blessings, Ben," he called over his shoulder. "It was good to see you."

"Have you heard from Charlie?"

"Charlie?" he asked.

"Charlie Abercrombie," I said.

He turned around.

"Wasn't Charlie Abercrombie a friend of yours?"

"I would hope he still is!"

"Charlie's living in Concord."

"Concord is a lovely town!" he said.

"Though I don't recall which cell block."

"What was that?" he asked.

"I don't recall which cell block," I repeated. "Charlie got caught in a Ponzi scheme."

"I'm sorry to hear it," he said.

"So, is Charlie still a friend?"

Suddenly the victim, he shot back: "I thought you were my friend."

More unsettling than his righteous indignation was his having thought of me as his friend. Just as I once thought that as a member of my tribe, Beringer was mine. Maurice might have been right: there wasn't much difference between Beringer and me.

"You're trapped," I said. "Like the rest of us."

Beringer angrily looked back.

"It isn't that the church is any worse," I said. "It's that it should have been better."

"The system is a sham," I overstayed my welcome. "Shame on all of us."

"You're sounding a bit self-righteous," he said.

"I'm no better than anyone else."

"No, you're not," the Bishop seized the chance.

"And neither are you," I said.

As he offered his finely tailored back to me, I should have been offended. But my incredulity about the church was gone: I was no longer surprised by its hypocrisy or monumental irrelevance. Whatever blame it had tried to foist upon the world, the fault was finally its own—impaled on the spires of an empire that had spectacularly engineered its own demise.

With Beringer at work, rearranging the deck chairs on the Titanic, the rest of us, for all our hypocritical freedom, had been left to swim on our own. Even my father, with his blue-blooded friends, were nodding off together in the pews: tacitly commending to their progeny more comfortable places to sleep. If the truth had been staring us all in the face—that institutions have to take to survive—we had failed to see the irony that Jesus was its greatest victim of all.

"You said you thought you were my friend," I called, turning him around a final time. "A friend is someone you would trust to set your piton. You put it through your brother's heart."

# 38

"I THOUGHT YOU MIGHT be back! Yeah," he effervesced, standing up in the garden. His brown sackcloth habit was kempt, but worn, and his ruddy Irish face, freshly scrubbed. "By God," Joe exclaimed, "Has it been a year? What the hell brings you back, young fella?"

Expecting the predictable probing questions concerning my relocation, the only thing he asked, with a nod of his head, was to remind him of my name. When I told him I was living across the valley in the foothills of the Albères, he perceptively observed that they were considered "'sauvage', which is ideal for a guy like you!" I immediately broached the possibility of helping at the monastery; and with bright-lit blue eyes, Brother Joe exclaimed, "You're gonna' taste the brothas' wine!"

So marked the start of a monastic rhythm that carries me to this day: writing in the morning; tending the garden and the vineyard in the afternoon; cleaning; chopping vegetables; washing pots and pans; and setting the table for the evening; and dining with the brothers and "clochards" from the mountains long into the psalmody of night. And sometimes late at night, when our guests would retreat back into the mountains—with the brothers fast asleep after one more day of being overtaken by the years—I would go out to my car and grab the silver flask, topped with Armagnac, and together we would sit under the skies lit like Joe's eyes, and talk about what we'd do tomorrow. Or sitting in the freedom of my chosen solitude, I would remember what Père Noël once said: "Solitude is being alone by your own choice—loneliness, by someone else's."

Whether Père Noël had another name, only "Père Noël" did him justice. His long, white beard, and elf-like countenance, was the picture of Father Christmas. Ensconced on Saturdays at the Picasso fountain against the Medieval rampart—where he magnetically attracted the children of Céret as parents shopped the weekly market—Père Noël had fled the German occupation for the safety of the "Zone Libre," and migrated south to the warmth of Roussillon and a room on Place de la République.

Père Noël had been a philosophy professor before losing his job at the Sorbonne. Fluent in English, he was famously involved in the underground French Resistance, and spent the rest of his life paying the price for the difficult choices he had made. I will always remember an insight he once shared at the close of the Saturday market: "You are spiritually homeless long before you are ever physically homeless."

When I asked if he was homeless, Père Noël replied, "I have a house—but I have no home. In the ancient world," he ruminated, "the only fate worse than death was exile."

Thanks to that fleeting conversation I felt like a homesick kid, when at dusk our diners left the dinner table for parts unknown to sleep. I knew it was all the aging brothers could do to make dinner at the end of every day. Increasingly haunted by ghosts of homelessness as I went to bed each night—once, startled awake by a flock of pigeons being stolen from the Esplanade—I couldn't help but wonder what it must be like, even in this temperate climate, to aimlessly wander out into the night, knowing that you had no home.

I remembered the terror as a trembling eight-year-old, which I would bring upon myself in bed, peering at the light beneath the bedroom door, that always seemed to be receding, where I would think about infinity, and then eternity, until I couldn't take it anymore—before submitting one last, unbearable time, to yet another million years more. A million years, and then a million-million years, and then a million-million-million years, until I would succumb to the all-consuming darkness, and the fear I was all alone. Still, relief was always just beyond the door, in the warmth of the living room, where my father and mother were there to reassure me that I would always be their son.

What must it be like to know there is no light beyond the bedroom door? What must it be like to be told goodbye, and sent into the swallowing darkness—with nothing between you and the eternal Pyrenees, rolling on into the night? What must it be like to know the home you left was no longer the home from which you came, where, except your broken family, scattered to the winds, no one could remember your name?

Like a spoiled undergraduate, I phoned my father to ask for money from home. I told him that fifty thousand francs should do it, and that he could count on me to put up half. Horse-trader that he was, after several rounds, peppered with fatherly complaints—"Your half! What about putting up mine?" and, "You don't know a damn thing about building!"—a wire was on its way to the Western Union office in nearby Perpignan, and Ben Sr., to the York Village Hardware Store, and then his Boston travel agent.

Seeking the lure for how best to catch an episcopal fisherman, I let out Brother Joe's finest line: "On a dry fly, he won't be disappointed." It didn't take long for Gentry to reply to the seven-day aerogramme. Convincing him that May was a stellar stretch for fishing, and the month of the cherry harvest, I was able to engage three Céretan masons to endure our help in the venture.

Maurice didn't respond to my shameless bribe of a pair of airline tickets. Having sent the details—including when and where he should be able to find Henri—I suspected that his workload, which I knew too well, made the trip unfeasible. Still, I envisaged him eying my proposal and shaking his Quebecois head: reassured that his former colleague had gone crazy, and it was better I had gone there alone.

My father arranged to meet Gentry's flight which was scheduled to connect through Boston, whence they would travel to Barcelona, where I would pick them up. But the preceding day I received a call that their itinerary had changed—they were being rerouted through Montreal, and arriving several hours later. Revving up the aged microbus which I had bought for monastic chores, on the first bright Saturday in May I was standing outside Spanish customs.

Sure enough, there they were, laughing as they came through the sliding customs doors. My father looked ready to wield a hammer, and Gentry, the fly rod in his grip. Catching sight of me, Ben Sr. waved, then unexpectedly turned around—as if he suddenly remembered something he'd inadvertently left behind.

And there was Henri, sporting a new backpack, his hair cascading to his shoulders. Before I could put one and one together, Maurice blew through the customs doors—rushing to catch his traveling companion as though they had been touring for years. In uncharacteristically casual attire, Maurice flashed his porcelain smile like a man who, for all his relentless cynicism, had finally been found out.

Maurice confessed that my aerogramme had piqued his curiosity. If he gave me credit for finding Henri, I paid for Henri's lack of a passport, which apparently demanded Maurice's connections to execute the document on time. When Maurice reached Gentry in Nova Scotia, the Bishop got in touch with my father, and together they engineered the travel plan that consolidated the foursome.

It would be hard to imagine a more motley crew, snoring up the cottage every night, and rising in the morning to a round of dirt cafés, brewed in my two-man pot. As hard as we worked from eight to five, the two-hour lunch was religion—when Henri and Maurice took the Francophonic lead with our trio of Catalan masons—battling French politics, local wine, and Catalan independence, to the deferential, often clueless nods of the less linguistic rest of us. Though I knew Brother Joe had been a boxer, in his sixties he remained a rock, hauling stones and mixing limestone mortar like a man who was about to turn thirty.

In two weeks, twelve erstwhile cattle stalls were returned to monastic cells—fully renovated and ready to accept electricity and a bed. We even re-pointed the limestone walls and hearth of the refectory and refurbished the massive rough-hewn table where dinner was served each night. What nine men accomplished in a fortnight of work could only have been described by Brother Joe's frequent, incredulous sighs: "By God, it's a miracle . . ."

# 39

As THE END OF our working days drew near, melancholy weighed in the air. I could tell my father was missing my mother and was ready to go home, and I sensed in Maurice the familiar burden of returning to the office. Given that Gentry didn't have a chance to cast a line in the Tech, he asked if he could return in a month "to allow you to make good on your promise."

At the final meal I asked Brother Joe to preside in memory of Hale, explaining Hale's technique of spontaneously retelling the story of the Last Supper. Joe happily obliged my spontaneous request "to bless our suppa' togetha'!" A far cry from Hale's fluid presentation, Brother Joe took liberties that managed to stun even the veterans of Cathedral in the Night.

Gathering us around the dinner table in the cavernous refectory, Brother Joe embarked on a vision of Jesus that made him look like he was from Rhode Island. He began by recalling how, the night before he died, Jesus brought his friends together to celebrate "those memorable years of sacrifice, and most of all, advencha.'" When he recounted the gruesome moment on the cross, Joe's voice suddenly cracked—finally pronouncing: "And by God, didn't he choose to win one for the Gippa'!"

I watched Henri straining to follow Brother Joe's parochial narrative—either wincing with pain, or with curiosity about what the hell a "Gippa" was. It came as no surprise that Quebecois Henri had never heard of 'Knute Rockne', nor quarterback, George Gipp, whose deathbed admonition still rings through the American ages: "I've got to go, Rock. It's all right. I'm not afraid. Some time, Rock, when the team is up against it, when things are wrong and the breaks are beating the boys, ask them to go in there with all they've got and win just one for the Gipper. I don't know where I'll be then, Rock. But I'll know about it, and I'll be happy."

Dinner was as raucous as the two weeks had been, complete with "the brothas' wine." With Maurice and my father at the dinner table, it wasn't at all surprising that the conversation turned to politics on both sides of the border. As my father was bemoaning our current President—"He wasn't even much of an actor!"—Maurice looked up as though he had something urgent that he needed to say.

"We have a new Mayor!" Maurice announced. He went on to impart that, following the Mayor's defeat by a progressive candidate, he decided to write an editorial on panhandling in Montreal. The letter got the incoming Mayor's attention, and along with several of his cronies, Maurice was asked to explore how best to address the problem from the street.

When I asked what he wrote, in typical form, Maurice held us all captive: "I just said, 'What's a buck to most of us? These guys provide an invaluable service!' I said, 'Some of my best conversations are out on Sainte Catherine Street!' Hell," Maurice blustered, "it's a small price to pay! My neighbors won't even talk to me!"

With dessert on the table, what I feared was going to happen finally did. By the end of the first week, Henri had effectively become the monastery chef—to the unquestioned gastronomic benefit of its growing number of patrons. As a former chef in a Montreal kitchen, the dinners approached "gourmet," thanks to his liberal use of herbs and spices that the brothers knew nothing about.

Before sitting down to his own crème brûlée, Henri was already talking at Maurice. After several minutes I went over to discover that Henri had "decided" to stay. Maurice tried to explain the laws by which Henri had to abide, to which Henri responded with outright indignation, "C'est mon chez moi!"—"This is my home!"

When Maurice appealed to me to back him up, I managed to maintain my composure. Excusing ourselves from the dinner table, I convened a legal huddle in which we both agreed that if anyone could get away with staying, it was someone who was homeless. In the spirit of, "What the customs boys don't know won't hurt 'em," Brother Joe struck a deal whereby Henri would live in one of the rooms in exchange for running the kitchen.

Maurice, Gentry, and my father headed home from Barcelona as planned. Before Maurice passed through the security gate, I exacted a promise from my friend; and reading the twinkle in his Quebecois eye, I suspected that one day he would return. What was most wrenching was saying goodbye to my faithful, unflagging father—but knowing he was planning to visit with my mother, I was able to let him go.

Coming back through the mountain pass that transected France and Spain, as the intoxicating air and magic of the evening was falling into night, I looked across the valley, filled with the orgiastic rhythm of the cricket's song, and was suddenly overwhelmed by the realization that I was home. Drowning in a sense of gratitude I hadn't known since my days as a pirate, I climbed the wooden stairs and sidled the length of the mezzanine to my bed. There, on my pillow, was a folded piece of paper torn from a spiral notebook, which I opened to the almost legible scrawl that could only have been a lawyer's.

*Dear Ben,*

*As you know, though I was always a good churchman, I never considered myself religious. To this day I believe that at heaven's gate, Mom will be in on the first ballot, while you and I will be smoking outside as Saint Peter equivocates. I can only thank you for all you endured to see through to what really matters.*

*As a thoroughgoing evolutionist, I don't know how I missed it—that for all that is bound to go wrong in this life, somehow it always ends up going right. Even when life dies, however tragically, it finds another way to live. I just read an article about how trees "communicate"—how the larger "mother trees" send out carbon to help smaller trees survive—giving me to wonder if, thanks to science, one day we will see that life is finally not about competition, but about cooperation.*

*I think I always had an affinity for Jesus—if not for the one I met in church. It was for the man of inconceivable courage that no one seemed to talk about. A courage I imagine in your friend, Luke Hale, and a courage I imagine in you, if only you don't get discouraged when everything seems to be going wrong.*

*Because freedom means life is free to go wrong. But it is also free to go right. And love is only love when it is freely given—otherwise it isn't love.*

*As you probably know, one of my favorite lines attributed to Twain goes something like: "When I was fourteen, my father was so ignorant that I could barely stand to have him around, and when I got to be twenty-one I couldn't believe how much the old man had learned in seven years." I hope someday you will say the same thing. If the sins of the father are visited on the son, it is only the son who can redeem them.*

*All my love,*
*Your Devoted Dad*

# 40

IN THE ENSUING WEEKS before Gentry returned, I would arrive in the early afternoon, with Henri faithfully at work in the kitchen and Brother Joe out in the garden. As often as I'd watched him gaze across that valley, it was a wonder that he never got enough—as though he were searching for a distant past, somewhere beyond the azure sea. Intoxicated by the pungent garrigue that permeates the south of France, and the sun, and the wind of the Tramontane that might as well have lasted a lifetime, I would stand at his back on the ancient promontory, where eternity collapsed into a moment, for me to consider, across our span of years, that elusive destination called home.

I finally braved my lingering question: "What are you looking for?"

Joe laughed. "At my age, I'd better have found it!"

"What have you found?" I asked.

Cocking his big Irish head, he mused, "The old Celts used to believe there was places on earth that were especially thin. Places where heaven and earth came near—places where they even collided.

"These days," he went on, gazing to the distance, "gettin' olda' can feel like gettin' thinna.'"

"Are you afraid of dying?"

He pensively smiled. "No, I can't say that I am."

"What do you think . . . it will be like?" I asked.

He knew what I was asking. Looking out again to the azure sea, he said, "Not that different from right now."

"So . . . what are we supposed to do until then?"

He said, "Think of it as now."

"Whatever I do now—never seems to be enough."

My plea caught Brother Joe's attention. Turning from his beloved sea, he said, "Ben, no one's keepin' score."

"I've spent my whole life keeping score," I said.

"Has anyone won?" he asked.

I laughed. "Not yet!"

"Maybe," he replied, "because in the end, there is no end."

With Henri at the helm, it was sometimes a challenge to keep the peace before dinner. Though I knew not to venture into the kitchen after three o'clock, Brother Joe remained blissfully ignorant of Henri's territorial limits. During Brother Joe's inaugural week of presiding at Hale's "Eucharistic meal," Henri so frequently cringed that Brother Joe agreed to deliver it in English.

The anger I once felt toward the suspects I had tried a thousand times in my private court of judgment, began to wane with the passage of time, in all its inherent wisdom. It wasn't that I felt any less offended by what they all had done: the Beringers, the Hollingsworths, the Wes Westmorelands, the Brooks's, and the Charlie Abercrombies. It was that I came to realize they were struggling no less than I—in a doomed attempt to supersede the riverbanks in order to get to the sea.

The truth is, these days I struggle to remember who is living and who is dead. I wonder if this was what his followers meant when they spoke of Jesus's "resurrection": that by remembering their friend, his death came to a life that was destined to change the world forever. It may have been more than empty metaphor that Jesus walked through walls and on the water—conjuring a presence more real than any dream that any of us had ever dreamed.

So, I had to wonder if I had spent my life looking in all the wrong places. Far beyond the church, I had submitted to walls that only acted to divide—rather than surrendering to this vast creation as the singular way to thrive. It was Hale who knew that God was a river which infused the whole of creation; it was Hale who knew that rather than let it pass him by, he had to jump in.

Because thanks to Hale, the world had changed, and it would never be the same again. Nor would its future, which always owes itself to an equally infinite past. As random as had been my first encounter with "Cathedral in the Night"—as I strolled the Old City, a prosperous attorney, enjoying his privileged life—in about the same time as Jesus's ministry, its course ineluctably changed: carrying me down a river of life which was destined to flow into the sea.

None of what happened in these last several weeks could have happened without Hale. Not the shelter, not the evenings of gourmet Eucharists, not the resurrected life of Henri, could have happened without Hale's own resurrected life—which depended upon his absence—convening a communion of six lonely men, who changed the world forever.

When Gentry arrived in Barcelona and bolted through the customs doors, it was as though he had left those heartrending months back across the Atlantic. As he was charging toward me, with his fly rod tube tucked underneath his arm, I realized how much I had missed my friend in the weeks that he was gone. But by the time his duffle bag appeared on the belt, he was caught up on all the news, including Henri's daily complaints about Joe's unpredictable antics.

For the next three weeks we piled into the bus with our lunches and fishing gear, and climbed to the Tech, high in the mountains, to cast the afternoons into the evenings. I couldn't help but marvel how, despite our shared regrets which were enough to kill a man, thanks to Hale, our once laden spirits had no choice but to rise again. And as I watched Gentry casting in the distance, high up in the mountains—with that rhythmic, arcing, evolutionary sweep that somehow always finds its target—I wondered how, for all the dispiriting sadness that should have decimated the world, we continue to pursue its irrepressible life, which continues to make no earthly sense.

It was the night before Gentry was going home when he asked what I hadn't dared to ask. With the trout grilled and eaten, and the second bottle drunk, the valley was aglitter at our feet. Looking out across the ancient Vallespir, baptized in the cricket's song, and the insistent staccato of the sensuous cicada, chirping in the falling night, it was as though a single question was organically destined to be asked by the voices of creation—through the darkness of a world that was waiting for an answer to be brought to its inexorable light.

"So, have you seen him?"

"Yes," I said.

"Where was he?"

"North Africa," I said.

"Are you sure?"

"Yes," I said.

"How do you know?" he asked.

"The night after you left, a Scirocco unexpectedly blew up from the Sahara. It doesn't happen often that the storm comes up a thousand miles from North Africa. When I got up in the morning and came out onto the terrace, everything was covered in red dust."

It was as though a palpable sigh of relief exhaled from Gentry's body. As he gazed across the shimmering valley, and into the eternal night, I wondered if his spirit had already departed for the northern coast of Morocco. Because whether it was Hale, or eternal life, or the red sand of the Sahara, there was an infinite sphere whose center was everywhere, and whose circumference was nowhere.

"He once asked if I knew why the nomadic Berbers haven't advanced in thousands of years."

"What did he say?"

"He said . . . 'because they had everything they needed.'"

"Because Hale had everything he needed," I came back.

"Everything, but a father."

I allowed him his grief, before my last appeal. "Do you remember," I asked, "the conversation we had that evening in your office? I interrogated him about the church's claim that Jesus was God's only son."

Gentry burst into laughter. "He said the three of us were God's only son!" he howled.

"For everything that happened," I said at last, "you let him know he was an only son."

Closing his eyes, perhaps with contentment, it was as if he were trying to remember. "I never . . . thought about it before," he said. "Maybe because I never knew it. But I really only felt like my father's son when I knew my brother felt the same way."

Eternal night stretched across the valley to the sea. He opened his eyes to the numinous sky in the light of the rising moon. Whether or not there were tears in his eyes didn't seem to matter anymore.

"So, what is one—plus one—plus one?" I hearkened back.

As if for the joy, he said, "One."

So it would be mine to keep watch from a distance for the red sands of the Sahara, as the eternally present, perpetually eroding mandala it had always been. However I wished to see Hale again, I knew it wouldn't be as a priest. Because I knew he was gone, that he wasn't coming back—that he'd gone on, downriver to the sea.

I even wonder if this sorry-looking journal is but one more evolutionary trace of a pentimentic life which seems always to be longing for ever greater redemption. Like brushstrokes on a canvas that summon one more stroke to realize its destined vision, the truth on the surface of any work of art is owed to what lies beneath. If every present moment is just an accident that vindicates a certain past, maybe the future is no less and no more than an anamnestic destiny.

So I can't forget my destined vocation as "Protector of the Animals," and far from the Esplanade, how I have no choice but to take it up again in these mountains. Still, there are times when I dream of a big, drafty house filled with "only sons and daughters," and of one day watching them in my father's lap, and hearing them call my mother, "Nanny." But I no longer wonder why my heart would break when those ogling pigeons were abused—knowing that every cell of creation is longing to be reconciled.

As I sit, taking in this panoramic world that turns evening into undulating night, drawing my eyes from garnet, to magenta, to the last remaining traces of light, I watch the valley rising before me to remind me of the ashes to which I will return: the evolutionary dust of a material world that is destined to bear new life again. So, every evening, before I retire to my shepherd's cottage to sleep, I remember in the midst this material world, the spirit that is destined to last. And lying in bed before the French doors to the sea, or aloft above the glittering vale, I know, if for a moment, this always dying present turns on an eternal past.

If the truth were known, I go to bed each night in great anticipation of the morning, and when I awake to the promise of the morning, I can't wait for the coming of the night. I seem only to remember rising to the sun that generously lights each day, and look forward to the grandeur of the glimmering night that promises to bear me to tomorrow. And I wonder if this is what heaven is like: an irrepressible hope for tomorrow, which intimates a future whose unending promise is borne in an eternal moment.

And I imagine the Cistercian monasteries, swept across sunbaked fields, holding centuries of dust and light and sleep, and chanting that is verging on rejoicing. And sometimes late at night, when I cannot sleep above the vast, illumined valley at my feet, I think I hear the brothers on the far side of Céret, singing through the solitary night. Yet it doesn't seem to matter if the brothers are asleep as I am sitting out on the terrace, because I know, for all my failures and regrets, that they are chanting just for me.

So I look forward to when Gentry returns, and as we fish high in the mountains, we remember that enigmatic, renegade priest who unwittingly changed the world forever. Maybe then we'll sit out on the terrace in the evening, with his sterling flask and endless talk, and host a nightlong banquet on an open fire, partaking of the trout we both had caught. And maybe then we'll drink from my poor stash of local wine, which is cheap and red and probably not good and tell of how the next time we would do it all again, and know that we would do it all again.

CPSIA information can be obtained
at www.ICGtesting.com
Printed in the USA
FSHW021634290321
79946FS